The Other Side of the Story

The Other Side of the Story

A Fun New View for Adults

Geoff Skinner

With Illustrations by Amy Skinner

FIRST EDITION

978-1-80541-879-5 eBook
978-1-80541-880-1 Paperback

To Michael and Bernie

for their smiles and encouragement

Table of Contents

1

Project Review

- Well, Gabriel, we haven't talked for a while. How's the project progressing?
- *Oh, getting there, Big J, getting there.*
- Yes – I received your report a week or so ago.

– *Good.*

– I've had a chance to review it and there are just a few points that you, as project manager, may be able to clear up for me.

– *Sure – go ahead.*

– Well, for a start, there seems to be a bit of duplication in the design.

– *Oh?*

– Yes, well, first of all, there's two eyes.

– *I can explain that.*

– Then there's two nostrils, two ears, two testicles on the male and two tits on the female.

– *Backup.*

– Oh?

– *Yes, in case one fails, there's always going to be a spare.*

– Hmm...

– *As for the tits, there's always the possibility of babies in future. Twins?*

– Ah!

– *You did tell us that we had an unlimited budget.*

– That's true. But, moving on, what's this little knot in the middle of its belly?

– *Just a vestige of the birth – "Man born of woman", and all that.*

– Yes, but can't you make it heal over nicely?

– *Might not be that easy. I'll have a word with the torso project leader.*

– Yes, would you, please.

– *Sure.*

– Now, coming back to the tits – I understand what they're for, but why the nipples on the male?

– *Oh, the additional cost was very small, and we felt that in future generations there might be some that weren't sure which way they swing. Get me?*

– Hmm... OK – leave them on for now.

– *Righto.*

– Moving on – just an aesthetic point, I suppose – those feet – ugh.

– *What about them?*

– Well, not to mince words, they're fucking ugly!

– *But functional, eh? We had to make them tough, especially since we decided on the bipedal option.*

– Mmm... yes. I have to say I'm still a bit worried about that. Are you sure they're not going to keep falling over with only two legs?

– *Well, we looked at the four-footed option, as you know, but we thought that two would be more elegant – distinguish it from the animals etc, and free up the hands.*

– OK, but won't they be a bit unsteady?

– *We think we've got that sorted.*

– OK, I'll leave that up to you. A couple more points, though...

– *Yes?*

– On the male – the dick.

– *Mmm...*

– Dual purpose. I can foresee all sorts of nasty problems with that. I don't think I need to describe them to you.

– *It just seemed to be an opportunity to simplify the design and reduce costs.*

– But I told you that cost was not an issue.

– *OK, I'll talk to our designers. We may be too far down the road to do anything about that, though. I'll get them to do some simulations but, you know, it might be more convenient to keep it that way – and it may make the design of trousers easier, if they ever get round to wearing them.*

– I'll wait to hear the results of the tests.

– *I'll send them to you.*

– Oh, and by the way – what's this little appendage?

– *Let me see – er – I don't know. Our people call it the appendix.*

– What's it for?

– *I'll get back to you on that.*

– OK. Another thing – hair. Why have you put it on the head and hardly at all on the rest of the body?

– *No need – it's always warm here in the Middle East, and why risk having nits and fleas all over the body.*

– Good point. Right – just checking my notes. Oh, yes – the arseholes. Two of them?

– *Resilience/redundancy.*

– OK, but under the armpits?

– *Convenience. Can you imagine trying to wipe your bum without seeing what you're doing?*

– Well, like you, I don't have to wipe my bum.

– *No, but you can imagine...*

– I'm still not convinced. Find somewhere else to put them.

– *I'll talk to the team – anything else?*

– No – I think that's it. Oh, just one thing – have you thought of a name for them?

– *Well, I thought "Adam and Eve", but some of the team like "Arnold and Karen".*

2

Mutton

– Well, thanks for coming in, Mrs Shepherd.

– *OK.*

– So, I imagine you know what it's about?

– *Yes, I suppose so, but it seems like a bit of a storm in a teacup to me, really.*

– Well, I imagine Mary has told you about yesterday?

– *Yes, of course – it's about her little lamb, but I can't see what the problem was.*

– Little lamb?

– *Yes, well, we thought it might be interesting for the other children to pet a lovely little newborn lamb.*

– Ah. Perhaps she hasn't been one hundred percent honest with you.

– *She just thought it would be nice for them.*

– Unfortunately, it wasn't.

– *But all children love seeing a little lamb.*

– Is that what she told you? Well, that wasn't exactly true.

– *What do you mean?*

– It was actually a 350 pound Lincoln ram.

– *Are you sure?*

– Oh, yes. The police and the ambulance men took photos.

– *Oh.*

– And it was utterly out of control.

– *Er, didn't she have it on a lead?*

– For the first 30 seconds, yes.

– *So, er, what happened?*

– To be brief, it went totally berserk.

– *Oh, dear. I hope it didn't do any damage, at all.*

– Somewhat.

– *Well, what happened?*

– Well, at first it made the children laugh and play...

– *Ah!*

– But then it went crazy. It's a big animal, you know.

– *Yes – so, what was the damage?*

– Here's the list:

- Eight children in hospital with broken ribs
- Two with fractured pelvises.
- 14 broken desks
- and £2,000 – worth of damage to windows and other furniture.

– *Oh.*

– The School Board will be sending you a bill for the damage, and the parents of the injured children will be suing you separately.

– *Oh dear.*

– And, while you're here, there's one other thing.

– *Oh?*

– Here's a bucket and a shovel – our school janitor refuses to clear up 50 pounds of sheep shit.

3

Paedo Pan

– Please have a seat, Mrs Darling.

– *Thank you.*

– Well, thanks for coming to see us. This must have been an appalling few weeks for you.

– *Yes, it's been dreadful – thank goodness it's all over.*

– Are the children OK?

– *Yes, more or less. Wendy is a strong girl, although she's still rather naïve.*

– That's good. This must have been hard for all of you.

– *It certainly has. Strangely, I think Nana has taken it just as hard as the rest of the family.*

I believe she somehow feels she should have prevented it all from happening.

– Dogs are sometimes very sensitive.

– *Yes.*

– So, the reason I invited you in was to bring you up to date with the case.

– *Yes, thank you.*

– I was hoping you would be able to meet George Hook. He's been working under cover for months keeping Pan, or 'Paedo Pan', as the press call him, under observation. Pan has got a record as long as your arm, you know.

– *Yes. And I understand we've got a lot to thank Inspector Hook for.*

– He's a fine officer.

– *I'm sure.*

– So, what are the doctors saying about the long-term effect of the hallucinogenic drugs the children were given?

– *They're optimistic that they will be OK. They seem to be sleeping better now, anyway.*

– That's good. Kids are very resilient.

– *So what about the youngster, Pan?*

– Oh, he's safely locked up, pending the trial.

– *Good. Wendy tells me he's only a boy, though.*

– He's 53.

4

Smokin'

– Good morning, Your Majesty.

– *Ah, good morning, Sir Walter. Tell me about your recent voyage to the Americas.*

– It was a great success, Ma'am.

– *Splendid! I cannot wait to hear about it. I understand you have returned with some considerable riches, which I look forward to accepting.*

– Indeed, ma'am. Even as we speak, my men are delivering chests of native gold to your treasury at the Tower.

– *Most gratifying, and, I am told, you have returned with some other remarkable discoveries.*

– Absolutely, ma'am. My aides have brought some samples here for your delectation.

– *I am anxious to see them, Sir Walter.*

– Here, your Majesty: in this small package, is something the natives call tabako.

– *Fascinating – they look like little white cylinders. And what do the words "Capstan Full Strength" mean?*

– The native name, ma'am.

– *And what are they for?*

– Allow me to demonstrate. May I use this candle?

– *Of course – what are you doing?*

– I am 'lighting a fag', or 'sparking up', as the natives refer to it.

– *Good heavens!*

– And you, your Majesty – snout?

– *If I may...CHOKE...CHOKE...Fuck that!*

– I confess – they take a little getting used to. Try one of these menthols.

– *Er, no – I think I'll pass.*

– Well, may I show you this, ma'am?

– *Hmm – it's heavier.*

– Yes – it's called a potato.

– *I see. Which end do you light it?*

5

Their Very Own Monster

– The bairns at school say it's not safe to go near the Loch, these days, Pa.

– *Aye, son, they're probably right.*

– But we live right by the shore, Pa.

– *Aye, we do that, son.*

– So, do we have to be careful?

– *Aye, best keep oor heads down.*

– Are we in danger, then.

– *Not as long as we take care, son.*

– I'll do that, Pa.

– *See you do, son. So will I.*

– So, you're afeared, too, Pa?

– *Aye, I am that, son, mortal afeared.*

– Is that why you spend so much time in the 'Haggis and Tatties', Pa?

– *Aye, likely it is, son.*

– Pa.

– *Aye, son?*

– Ma's coming home from work soon. Can I come to the Haggis with you?

6

You're Fired!

- So, here we are, Mr Farynor.
- *Mmm.*
- I understand you have, or rather had, a baker's shop in Pudding Lane.
- *Er, yes.*
- And you were a little careless, the other evening?
- *I suppose so.*
- Mmm, I imagine you are aware of the extent of the damage?
- *Er, not really.*
- Well, I'll tell you. The fire destroyed:

- 436 acres of London
- 13,200 houses
- 85% of the historic city within the walls
- St Paul's Cathedral
- 87 other churches,

– and left 80,000 people homeless, not to mention several dead.

– What do you have to say?

– *...Er...sorry?*

7

A Christmas Cavil

Knock Knock

- Mr Scrooge – it's you!
- *That's right, Cratchit. A merry Christmas, everyone!*
- But, er, what brings you here?
- *Just to give you this!*
- Well, thank you. What a fine goose. Do come in.
- *Thank you.*
- Emily - look what Mr Scrooge has brought! Yes – we'll keep it for the weekend. Er, find a chair at the table for Mr Scrooge.

– *How kind. Good grief – I've never seen such a huge turkey!*

– Yes – it's corn-fed. Special order.

– *I love your decorations, and the huge tree!*

– We had it sent from Norway.

– *Covered in gifts, I see.*

– Mmm

– *And what's that under the tree?*

– Oh, it's a new bike.

– *Who's that for?*

– Tiny Tim.

– *Er, where is he?*

– Oh, he's in California for a couple of weeks. There's a surgeon there that can do wonders with crippled legs.

– *And was that a new carriage I saw outside?*

– Mmm. Anyway, how about an aperitif?

– *I don't mind if I do.*

– Negroni, or a vintage champagne?

– *Oh, the champers, I think.*

– There you go.

– *Thanks.*

– We were just about to have lunch. Would you care to join us?

– *I'd love to.*

– Foie gras? We had it brought over at the weekend.

– *Lovely...*

– Now – turkey? With all the trimmings, as they say.

– *I can't wait.*

– And I always find the best accompaniment is a fine premier cru Chablis. May I?

– *Please do......well, that was all excellent. I couldn't eat another thing*

– Oh, I'm sure you can make room for some Christmas pudding.

– *If you insist.*

– Cream or brandy sauce? I find it tastes best made with a 40-year-old cognac.

– *Very tasty.*

– Now, some more of that cognac, or a vintage port?

– *Oh, I think the port.*

– There you are...another?

– *I'd love to, but I really must get going.*

– Well, I'll see you after Boxing Day.

– *Er, no. In court, perhaps.*

– What do you mean?

– *Marley told me – you've had your hand in the till for more than a year.*

– Er...er...I was having some cashflow problems - I was going to pay it back. I promise.

– *Oh, you will...you will.*

8

A Close Shave

– Yes, Guv?

– *Short back and sides, please, mate.*

– Righto. Have a seat.

– *I've left it a bit long this time – sorry.*

– Not a problem, chief.

– *Good.*

– (Snip-snip) So, do you work locally?

– *Yes –I'm working just up the road.*

– (Snip-snip) For one of the papers, I suppose.

– *Yes – just started at the Daily News. That's why I've never been in here before.*

– (Snip-snip) I thought I hadn't seen you.

– *That's right.*

– (snip-snip) Family man?

– *No, actually – I'm single – live on my own. I like it that way, actually.*

– (Snip-snip) Oh – interesting. This your lunchtime, is it?

– *Yes – just got time for a quick trim and a snack.*

– (Snip-snip) Well, if you haven't eaten yet, I can recommend the pie shop, next door.

– *Thanks – I'll try it.*

– (Snip-snip).

– *What's – er – this big lever thing beside the chair?*

– (Snip snip) Oh, er – it's just to adjust the height.

– *Oh.*

– (Snip-snip) Got time for a shave, while you're here? You've got a lovely throat for a shave, if I may say so.

– *No thanks, I'm a bit pushed.*

– (Snip-snip) OK, if you're sure.

– *As a matter of fact, a friend of mine recommended me to you.*

– (Snip-snip) Oh?

– *Yes. Haven't seen him lately, though.*

– (Snip-snip) Oh, nice of him, anyway.

– *Actually, I wasn't too sure if he meant you or the chap on the other side of the pie shop.*

– Oh, what? Mr Tod?

– *Is that his name?*

– Yes. Well, there you go, guv. That'll be sixpence.

– *See you again, I hope – bye.*

9

A Crowded Forest

– So, thanks for coming in today.

– *Glad to be of assistance.*

– Well, here at the Nature Conservancy, we are always very concerned to protect the forest environment.

– *Of course.*

– ...and I need to understand if there has been any contravention of the forest bylaws.

– *Yes – I'm in favour of that, of course, so I'm pleased to help.*

– Well, let me start by saying that, as an honorary warden, you are not, yourself, under investigation in this situation. In fact, we are trying to protect your habitat as much as the wild animals and birds.

– *That's good to know.*

– So, can we start at the beginning – last Saturday night.

– *I remember it clearly – bloody nuisances.*

– OK - go on.

– *Well, the wife and I were hanging out with the girls. It was a lovely evening – peaceful enough until we started hearing voices.*

– Human voices?

– *Oh, yes.*

– And, of course, the forest is protected land. It's off limits after dark to anyone – except, of course, to you and your people.

– *I was well aware of that.*

– So, when you heard voices, what did you do?

– *Well, I sent my dogsbody to see what was going on.*

– And what did he tell you?

– *Frankly, he said, "Guv'nor, it's like Piccadilly Circus out there".*

– Oh?

– *Yes. He said there was a gang of scruffbags trying to rehearse some kind of performance. Why they had to do it in the woods, fuck knows.*

– Odd.

– *Yes – bunch of drongoes. One of them had even brought a phoney brick wall made out of plywood, with a hole in it.*

– What was that for?

– *Who knows.*

– So, who else was there, after dark?

– *Oh, a bunch of young yuppies from town – blokes and girls.*

– What were they up to in the woods?

– *What do you fucking think?*

– Oh, I see – so what did they actually do?

– *They were milling about, talking loudly, frightening the wildlife and generally misbehaving. A couple of them had bottles, of course.*

– I see. So, what did you think?

– *Well, it was too late to call you, so I decided to do something to scare them all off myself.*

– Don't worry, you're not in trouble; I'm grateful to you for trying to handle the situation; so, what did you do?

– *Well, to be frank, I was a bit pissed off with her indoors at the time.*

– Your missis?

– *Yes, Titty.*

– So, er...

– *So I decided to kill two birds with one stone.*

– Go on...

– *Well, with Pucky's help, I decided to take the piss out of the missis and frighten the crap out of the 'rude mechanicals'; oh, and to make fools of a couple of the yuppies too.*

– I see...

– *Long story short, Pucky and I gave one of the peasants a donkey's head and made Titty fall in love with him.*

– And...

– *Worked like a dream.*

– When was this?

– *Midsummer night.*

10

A Desert Island Tale

– Hi, Chacachacunatunapuna

– *Oh, hi, Lupu*

– Long time no see, mate.

– *Tell me about it!*

– Well, I heard you got kidnapped – you've been gone for a couple of years. So what happened?

– *All right – I'll tell you if you want to know.*

– Go on

– *OK. Well, me and some of the boys decided to go over to Coconut Island. You know – a few drinks, couple of laughs, barbie. We were going to snack on that guy they caught stealing*

– skinny bastard, but with a bit of marinade he would have been OK. So we were on the beach - lit a fire, fucking about – as you do. Suddenly this tall guy, red face, fur hat comes running up out of nowhere with a weird stick in his hand, points it at Fugu and BANG – Fugu falls down dead.

– Shit! What did you do?

– *What do you think – we fucking legged it, dinner too.*

– Did you get away?

– *Yes and no. At least, he didn't kill me, but he got the other three with his magic fire-stick, so I just threw myself down in the sand and waited for my turn.*

– Yeh?

– *Yeh. But instead of firesticking me, he's made me go to his hut with him. He went back to our boat and wrecked the bastard. Didn't even bother to snack on any of the lads – weirdo. Anyway, I could see I was fucked. So that's what I've been doing for the past four years – working like a bloody slave for old Furhat. In the end, one day, a bastard great canoe turned up, full of more pinkfaces and I managed to do a runner while he pissed off with them.*

– So when was that?

– *Just a couple of months ago. I'll tell you what, if you ever see a pinkface, mate, run, and when you get tired of running – keep fucking running.*

11

A Feast for Old Steven

– *All right, Siggy.*

– All right – I suppose.

– *Yeah? You look a bit fed up.*

– You could say that.

– *What's it all about?*

– Oh, you know...

– *Don't tell me. It's him again, I suppose – your guv'nor.*

– How did you fucking guess?

– *So what was it this time?*

– Last fucking night.

– *Go on.*

– We was in his chambers, about midnight - I'd just been putting his linen away, and he was wandering about, looking out the window.

– *Yeah?*

– Suddenly he says, "Sigismund – come here, will you. Look out the window".

– *What was it?*

– Well I looked out. You know what it was like last night. Freezing cold, two feet of snow and blowing a fucking blizzard.

– *I know – it was like bloody Siberia. So what did he want you to look at?*

– Well, I looked out, and there was this old peasant, up to his knees in the driving snow, picking up sticks.

– *Fuck that!*

– Yes. So, his nibs says, "Who's that? Where does he live?" I looked down and I could just see – it was that dirty old cunt that lives underneath the mountain. You know him – he lives right against the forest fence, by St Agnes' fountain.

– *That's more than a couple of miles away!*

– Yes. Fuck knows what he was doing up by the castle. There must be plenty of firewood in the forest.

– *Right!*

– Yeah - I should have said that to HM, but he never gave me a chance.

– *Why – what happened?*

– He's turned straight round and said to me, "Sigismund, be a good lad and go down to the kitchen and get a nice joint of beef, and then get a couple of bottles of wine from the cellar (not the good stuff – the stuff we serve to my in-laws). Then get a few armfuls of logs. We'll take them to him and watch him eat".

– *He's potty.*

– Oh yes – and I'd already cottoned on to what he was thinking about, but you don't answer back to the king of fucking Bohemia – not if you want to keep your job.

– *So what happened?*

– Well, he called down for a footman to get a little sledge, and told me to get my coat and meet him at the palace gates.

– *Fuck!*

– The old boy had pissed off by then, but the guv'nor wanted to take all the stuff to his house. I should have kept my fucking mouth shut.

– *Yeah – but you weren't to know.*

– No. I suppose not. So off we went. It was blowing a blizzard and about ten below zero. It was all right for him – you've seen that big fur coat he's got – and the fur-lined boots up to his fucking knees – but I was wearing these shoes – look, they're still fucking soaking – and my short coat. And guess who had to pull the fucking sledge. That's right – Joe Cunt.

– *At least that would have warmed you up.*

– Fuck off. In the end I had to say something. I said, "Sire, it's getting dark and the wind's getting colder. I've had it."

– *So what did he say?*

– He said, "Step in my footprints and stop moaning".

– *So did you?*

– Yes – a fat lot of fucking good that did.

– *So what happened?*

– Well, we got there in the end. The old boy didn't touch the wine – he was probably going to sell it, and Old Wence got bored in about five minutes – not even long enough for me to get warmed up. I don't know how I managed to get back, but we did, and he said, "Well done, lad. We have blessed the poor, and will ourselves find blessing. You may come in fifteen minutes late tomorrow morning". I felt like saying, "Thanks a fucking bunch", but I thought better of it.

– *What about the old peasant?*

– Oh – he was outside again today, pretending to pick up sticks. I asked Wence what he wanted me to do and he said, "Go down and tell him to piss off. What's he think this is – fucking Christmas"?

12

Wrong Address

– Congratulations, Admiral Columbus; we have finally reached India by the Western passage.

– *I knew we could do it. It has taken a voyage of many months, but I have never lost faith.*

– Nor have we, your crew – those of us who have survived – and we have at last stepped ashore.

– *Indeed, and I look forward to our first encounter with the local Indians.*

– I too.

– *While we establish an encampment here, I have already sent an exploratory party to venture inland to meet the native people.*

– Ah! Here they come now.

– Greetings, Admiral.

– *So – what do you have to report?*

– An interesting meeting with the local East Indians, Admiral.

– *Please tell me about it.*

– Well, we encountered a group of Indians, but communication was difficult. Our linguist tried to communicate in Hindi, Bengali, Tamil and Gujarati, but without success.

– *A pity – clearly the tribes on this side of India have a different culture.*

– Indeed, and unlike the dwellings that we know on the other side of India, they live in conical tents and subsist on a diet of roast buffalo.

– *Fascinating!*

– It seems that the culture and diet on this side of India are totally different from those with which we are familiar.

– *Pity – after that trip, I could murder a fucking curry!*

13

A Lavish Tale

– So, Thomas, thank you for coming in.

– *Well, I'm pleased that you seem to be so interested in my design.*

– We are, in fact we believe it could revolutionize internal sanitation.

– *That was my intention.*

– Well, in brief, we would like to take up your patent and begin production.

– *That's wonderful!*

– Our marketing people are carrying out a study to forecast demand but, at this stage, we are optimistic.

– *Excellent; so, how much are you offering to pay for the use of my patent.*

– Oh, as soon as we have some demand forecasts, we will make you an offer.

– *I see.*

– There's just one point we need to clear up with you, though.

– *Oh?*

– It's about the product name.

– *I see.*

– You have registered the patent under your own surname.

– *Yes.*

– Well, we should like to find a different name to market the product under.

– *Oh, that's a shame – I'd rather thought I could make a reputation for myself with this product.*

– I can understand that, but we thought we might come up with a name with more customer-appeal, Mr Crapper.

14

A Whirlwind Romance

– Hi, Shelley.

– *Oh, hi, Sluggish.*

– How's it going?

– *Slow, as usual.*

– Thought I saw you the other day, but you were feet away, so I didn't wave.

– *Oh, OK.*

– So, what's new with you?

– *Oh, same old, same old – what about you?*

– Something wonderful, as it happens!

– *Tell me about it.*

– Well, here it is – I'm in love!

– *Wow! But, er, you're like me – a hermaphro – thingy*

– Of course, but we can have feelings too.

– *So, er....*

– Well, you know the greenhouse at the end of the garden?

– *Bit out of my range, actually – it must be a day's crawl away. I'm not up to that kind of trip at my age.*

– Well, anyway, I was down there a few days ago and I tried to peep through one of the bottom panes.

– *So, what did you see?*

– An absolute sweetie!

– *You mean a reflexion?*

– Yes – it was gorgeous!

– *Oh dear!*

– I know I mustn't rush things – it's not going to be a whirlwind romance.

– *I can imagine. But you do know it was you, don't you?*

– Of course.

– *So, er...*

– Don't worry - I'm going to take it slow.

15

'Ark the 'Erald Angels

– Greetings, Noah.

– *Oh, Hi, God, long time no see.*

– No, I've been a bit busy with the moon and stars and stuff. So, how's the work progressing?

– *Oh, I'm quite pleased with it, actually.*

– Ah!

– *I've laid out some lovely lawns.*

– So I see.

– *And Shem's built some swings and a nice slide for the kids.*

– Er, good.

– *The football pitches are all laid out, too.*

– Football?

– *Yes, and some lovely changing rooms – showers and everything.*

– Showers, er...lovely.

– *The trees are going to take a while, but Ham's keeping them nicely watered.*

– Oh, dear.

– *The animals are going to love it here. We've got the rabbits and hedgehogs settled in already and the birds are all nesting nicely. Oh, and have you seen the duckpond – I'm rather proud of it.*

– Yes – I can hear them, er, lovely.

– *Yes, I'm very pleased with our progress.*

– Good, but can I just ask you a question?

– *Sure, Lord.*

– How's that mild deafness problem you used to have?

– *Oh, I manage to live with it; but let's get under this tree – it's starting to rain.*

– So it seems.

– *So, what do you think?*

– What do I think? I suppose I'm going to have to do this my bloody self, as usual.

16

Cowboys

– Yeehah!

– *What?*

– Yeehah!

– *What do you mean?*

– Nothing, pal – just celebrating.

– *Oh, er. I see.*

– So, you're a cowboy too, pal – like me.

– *I suppose so.*

– So, where do you drive your herd, partner?

– *Well, sometimes from this field to that one over there.*

– Oh, is that it?

– *No – each day we drive them into the shed for milking.*

– Milking?

– *Yes – don't you do that?*

– Nah – we're always on the move.

– *That must be a pain.*

– Er, not really – it's what we do.

– *Why?*

– Well, we have to drive them hundreds of miles to where the cattle markets are.

– *Why don't you have markets where the cows are?*

– Er...

– *Or why don't they raise cows where the markets are?*

– Well, I guess they wouldn't need cowboys then.

– *So?*

– Er, then we wouldn't have jobs and there'd be no-one to make cowboy films about.

– *Well, this is a fast-growing country. Couldn't you do something else?*

– No – we're cowboys.

– *Like me.*

– I guess.

– *Mmm.*

– And we face danger, too, out on the prairie.

– *Oh – what danger?*

– Indians.

– *Well, we have Indians, too, but they're mostly miles away, in Southall, and they're not dangerous.*

– Yes, but ours get angry because we're crossing their land.

– *So, why are you ... oh, forget it.*

17

The Oven's Secret

– Sit down, Gretel.

– *Why should I?*

– You're not in charge here – sit down!

– *Bastard!*

– All right. That's better. Now let's talk about old Frau Dinksbumps.

– *Never 'eard of 'er.*

– Oh, I think you have.

– *Yeh?*

– All right, let's talk about something else.

– *Talk about what you like.*

– What do you know about a chestful of gold?

– *We found it in the woods, me and Hansel.*

– Where, exactly?

– *Just in the woods.*

– In a little gingerbread house, by any chance?

– *I don't know what you're talking about.*

– Hansel has told us everything.

– *The little bastard! He's a liar!*

– OK, let me start again. What happened at the gingerbread house?

– *Nuffink. I don't know nuffink about no gingerbread house.*

– Oh, I think you do. I think you and your brother terrorized old Frau Dinksbumps until she told you where her gold was, and then you did away with her.

– *Prove it!*

– Fortunately, I don't need to. I've got your brother's confession.

– *'E's an arsehole. E'd say anything.*

– The only thing he wouldn't tell us is the whereabouts of the old lady.

– *What old lady?*

– Right. Let's try another question. What happened to the front door, and what are those sticky crumbs down the front of your blouse?

18

That Takes the Cake!

– Never again!

– *I can imagine.*

– Yes – never again. That's the last time I take in a lodger.

– *So, it didn't work out, then?*

– You could say that!

– *So, what made you take him in in the first place?*

– Well, he was the bloody king, so you don't like to say no.

– *Yes, I suppose so.*

– I thought he was just slumming – I never watch the news.

– *So, why did he come to you?*

– Well, I eventually found out he was on the run.

– *So, who was chasing him?*

– Oh, some bloody foreigners from up north.

– *Shit!*

– Yes. He said he was trying to 'regroup', but I never saw any signs of his bleeding 'group'.

– *So, was he giving you any rent?*

– You're having a laugh!

– *Oh, that's bad, but I suppose you can't really kick a king out.*

– Well, not without a bloody good reason.

– *So, did you come up with one?*

– Yes, eventually, thank goodness.

– *What happened, then?*

– Well, you know the wife's a bloody good pastry cook?

– *I know – I had a couple of her mince pies last Christmas.*

– Yes, well, she was knocking up a big order of fairy cakes for the local pastry shop. A lovely little earner for the week.

– *So?*

– She put them in the oven, but then she remembered she'd run out of icing sugar, so she needed to pop out to the shop to pick some up.

– *And?*

– So she says to Alf, "Keep an eye on those cakes. They need to come out in ten minutes if I'm not back". "OK, love", he says.

– *So, did he?*

– Did he bollocks! When she came back, the whole lot were burnt.

– *So..?*

– Well, she gave him an almighty rucking and slung him out.

– *I can imagine – I know your missis.*

– Yeh – good riddance.

– *I suppose you haven't heard from him since?*

– Not really, but I did hear he gave away half the country to the bloody Danes. Some fucking king!

19

EIEIOh Dear

– Good morning, Mr. MacDonald. Officer Jones, Ministry of Food and Ag.

– *Mornin'*

– Just a routine check, as you have been claiming a number of government subsidies for your livestock, and I just need to verify what animals you have.

– *Right-o.*

– Well, first of all, you are claiming an allowance for cattle. Exactly how many are there in your herd?

– *Just the one – one cow.*

– Oh, so you're largely a sheep farmer, then?

– *Koind of.*

– How large is your flock?

– *One – Woolly.*

– I see, so, er, pigs?

– *Snouty.*

– I think I'm beginning to get the picture. Goats?

– *Nanny.*

– Dogs?

– *Fido.*

– Cats? Let me guess. Not many rats and mice for it to catch, eh? Then there's the poultry. Tell me about them.

– *Quacker, Henny, Gobbler and Goosey.*

– Any other livestock? I notice you have a dovecote.

– *Lovie.*

– Lovie?

– *The dove.*

– I see. That's rather a lot of breeds you're claiming subsidies for.

– *Arr.*

– I make it eleven.

– *Arr.*

– And you're claiming separate subsidies for each species?

– *Arr.*

– How do you make a living?

– *Subsidies.*

– That's what I thought. So, you make an income and keep this big farmhouse totally on government subsidies for eleven animals, without working?

– *Arr – but you're wrong.*

– Oh?

– *You forgot Leslie.*

– Leslie?

– *The llama.*

20

Furry

– Hi, Goldie.

– *Oh, hi.*

– Nice coat. Must be a bit warm in this weather, though.

– *Yeh – but I don't mind. It makes me feel good.*

– What sort of fur is it?

– *Er, oh – fox, I think.*

– I must say, I always love your outfits. A bit eccentric, but, why not, eh?

– *I suppose so.*

– Remember those sealskin pants you used to have?

– *Yes, I've still got them somewhere.*

– And those bunny ears you used to wear at parties? HaHa!

– *Mmm.*

– And what about that black and white stripey outfit of yours!

– *Yes.*

– So – I hear you've joined a new 'common interest' group up in town. A hobby thing, is it?

– *Sort of.*

– What sort of things do you do?

– *Er, it's to do with animals.*

– Oh, what – you're animal lovers? I didn't know you had any pets.

– *I don't. It's not quite like that.*

– Oh?

– *It's sort of dressing-up and role-playing.*

– Sounds like fun.

– *It's a bit more serious than that – we're furries.*

– Fairies?

– *No, furries. You wouldn't understand – it's more of a way of life thing.*

– Oh, I've heard about that. But it's all only pretend, eh? You lot don't really imagine you're animals?

– *Er... of course not.*

– Sort of play-acting, eh?

– *Er... sort of, for some people.*

– So, anyway, what else is new? I heard you were thinking of moving. Did that happen?

– *No – I'm still in the village.*

– Oh, right. Someone told me you were going to live with some friends in the woods – mother, father and a baby. So that didn't happen, then?

– *No, it didn't work out.*

– Shame. Family, was it?

– *I'd have liked to think so.*

– Oh, OK. Anyway, I must get going. Love the big boots, by the way. Look a bit like chicken feet!

– *Thanks. Cluck...cluck.*

21

Grand Larceny

– *Hi, George. Haven't seen you down at the Ogre's Arms lately.*

– No – I've been giving it a bit of a miss the last week or so.

– *Oh – why's that? The boys have been asking about you.*

– Yeh, well, I've had to keep an eye on the castle lately.

– *Why – what's the problem?*

– Fucking burglars.

– *Oh no!*

– Yes - bastard kids – or one in particular.

– *You know who it is, then?*

– Oh, yes.

– *Is he local?*

– No – he's from 'Down Below'

– *The cheeky little sod. How did he get up here, though?*

– You'll never believe it. He's a yokel from the village. Apparently he swapped a cow for a bag of beans and they turned out to be magic.

– *They'd bloody need to be, to be worth a fucking cow.*

– Yeh, not that he worked that out himself – the little dimwit.

– *Don't tell me – he climbed up that beanstalk that's growing in your back garden.*

– And the rest, mate.

– *You mean he's burgled your place more than once?*

– Yes – the cheeky little bastard.

– *What did he take?*

– Oh, just cash, the first time.

– *How much did he get?*

– Only a bag of gold, that's all.

– *Blimey! So what else?*

– He came back and got my chicken.

– *Not the one that lays the golden eggs?*

– Yep.

– *Fuck! The little sod. But how do you know who it was?*

– That's the worst part.

– *Go on.*

– You've met my missis, haven't you?

– *Yes – small woman. I've always wondered how, er...*

– Yes, well, never mind that. You know how soft-hearted she is – and she's got the brain of a bleeding guppy. She actually caught him sneaking in and he told her some sob-story about his widowed mum starving to death and how he got the beans, and she felt sorry for him, so when I came home she hid him in the oven.

– *You're kidding.*

– I had an idea there was someone around – I've got a nose for that kind of thing, so I gave it the old "Fee fi fo fum" but she said "Don't be silly, George, there's no-one here," so I let it slide.

– *As you would.*

– It wasn't till the next morning I found somebody had fucked off with my gelt! I went fucking mad!

– *So what did she say?*

– Not a word.

– *So when did he come back?*

– A couple of days later!

– *What happened?*

– The same thing – the silly cow. Bastard took my chicken, and I still didn't cotton on. That's when she admitted what she'd done. Full waterworks of course, and "I'm so sorry, George".

– *So what did you do?*

– You mean before or after I finished kicking the shit out of her?

– *That goes without saying.*

– I decided to stay indoors – keep a low profile for a few days, in case he comes back.

– *What d'you think he'll be after, next time?*

– Oh, I know exactly what he'll have his eye on.

– *The harp! Your self-playing golden harp!*

– Exactly. But this time I'll be waiting for the little swine! I've told the harp, and she'll scream blue murder if someone tries to nick her.

– *Good for you. That should do it*

– I'll have him, even if I have to climb down the bloody beanstalk after him.

– *Well, good luck, mate. You can tell us all about it when you get back in the pub.*

– Oh, I will. Don't worry, I will.

22

Hands-off

- Well, Mrs Beeton, may I first congratulate you on the well-deserved success of your cookery book.
- *Thank you. I am most pleased with the interest it has generated.*
- As, perhaps, the first of its kind, it has captured the hearts of many middle-class ladies.
- *So I understand. That has been my hope.*
- I imagine a great deal of research went into the book's preparation.
- *Oh, yes. I talked to a number of cooks during its development.*

– I'm sure – but good cookery involves a lot more than simply following a recipe, doesn't it?

– *Absolutely.*

– So, did each recipe require you to carry out a lot of experimentation?

– *What do you mean?*

– Well, you must have spent many hours in your kitchen.

– *Er, certainly not.*

– Oh?

– *Well, I am an upper middle-class English lady. I do not ever enter my kitchen – I have staff for that purpose.*

– Umm... of course... so, er, what general advice would you offer to your readers regarding home cookery?

– *Oh, to take great care and demand full references when employing a cook – and be sure she can read and write.*

23

The New Constitution

– Hi Maurice.

– *Oh, hello Izzy.*

– Have you heard, then?

– *No. What?*

– About the Old Man.

– *What about him?*

– He's back!

– *What, from up the mountain?*

– Yes!

– *Well, there's a surprise; I thought he was gone for good – it's been weeks.*

– I know.

– *I mean, when I saw him on the way up there with nothing but a hammer, a cold chisel and a pack of sandwiches, I thought he'd finally flipped.*

– Far from it – he's been working on a set of laws, all carved out in stone (literally!). He's put them on display so we can all read them.

– *Well, that's great; about time – I've always said we need some laws. The judges seem to make them up as they go along. What side of the track you're supposed to ride your camel, for instance; there's been some nasty accidents with that.*

– No, no. They're about important stuff.

– *You wouldn't say that if your arse was covered with hoofprints. I've been there.*

– No – they're serious stuff – you know, lifestyle.

– *Like what, for instance?*

– Well, I can't remember the exact words. But there's ten of them. I'll go through them for you, if you like.

– *Go on, then.*

– Well, the first one is, "Don't have any gods before Big J".

– *That's no problem – who needs them? I suppose you can have other gods as long as he's the boss, then?*

– I imagine so.

– *That's no problem, then. What's next?*

– "Don't make any kind of image and pray to it".

– *No prob. Who'd want to? Frankly, I never pray anyway (except on the occasional tribal lottery day.)*

– He's very tough on it, though. It's not only you that gets punished – the next four generations of your family get done for it, as well.

– *Yes, but who'd be prat enough to carve a dummy of a woman, say, or, I don't know, a square or a cross and pray to it.*

– You're right.

– *So what else – anything about arson or fraud or getting pissed or beating up your missis?*

– Funnily enough, no.

– *Thank fuck for that.*

– No, but we're not allowed to swear.

– *Fuck. Sorry, I mean gosh.*

– No, that's OK, you just have to avoid putting God's name in the expression. I imagine 'gosh' is borderline, though, so be careful.

– *I can cope with that. What else?*

– Well, the next one was, "Don't work on a Saturday".

– *It's sounding better and better. What about Sundays?*

– Not mentioned, but I imagine you can take it easy then as well. Anyway, the next one is, "Be nice to your mum and dad".

– *Hmm... You've met my old lady. It's going to be a struggle.*

– You'll manage. Just stay away a lot.

– *I do. What's next?*

– "Don't kill people."

– *D'uh! I think we already had some idea that might be a bit naughty.*

– Yes. Then, I think, it's, "Don't put yourself about if you're married".

– *Well, I'm not, but you don't have to be a genius to see that that can cause a lot of problems.*

– Then, "Don't nick stuff".

– *Are you telling me it took a couple of months for him to come up with this shit?*

– Now you mention it, it does seem a bit, er, obvious.

– *I would say so.*

– There's two more.

– *Do fucking tell.*

– "Don't try to fit anyone up for something he didn't do."

– *Well, you'd have to be a bit of an arsehole. I rather think we could have figured that out for ourselves.*

– Mmm... well, the last one, I think, was, "Don't covet anything belonging to someone else".

– *What's 'covet'?*

– It means we're not supposed to want it.

– *Well, how can you help it? And, anyway, who'd know unless we try to do something about it – and I imagine that would probably be covered by one of the other rules.*

– I don't know – I'm just telling you what the stone said.

– *Well, as far as I can see, it's a bit of a non-event. Where's the Old Man now, by the way?*

– I think he's having a bit of a lie-down. I think something in those sandwiches disagreed with him.

– *I think I'll have a lie-down, too. I'll have a look at the stone tomorrow.*

24

Please Await Further Information

– Well, good morning, Mr Stephenson.

– *Good morning.*

– A historic day, I'm sure you would agree.

– *I believe so.*

– Oh, I am confident that we are, today, entering a new era in the field of passenger transport.

– *That is my hope.*

– The first demonstration of a non-horse-drawn vehicle that will revolutionize passenger transport throughout the civilized world!

– *Yes – I must confess to some excitement and satisfaction.*

– Oh, justifiably so – as the inventor of the first means of steam-driven land transport...

– *Yes.*

– ...and you must be hugely gratified by the hundreds of people who have turned up to witness this historic event.

– *Of course – I am most excited and flattered.*

– I understand that there will be as many as thirty passengers on this thrilling initial rail journey.

– *I believe that is so.*

– Yes – I see them there, already assembled on the platform, ready to be a part of this historic journey. Celebrities, all of them.

– *Yes – I am delighted that they have consented to take part.*

– ... not to mention the vast crowd of people gathered here to witness this epoch-making event. But I see your engine-driver approaching. I believe he wishes to have a word with you.

– *Yes – please excuse me for a moment.*

– ...

– So, what can you tell us about this historic journey?

– *Bad news, I'm afraid*

– Oh, no!

– *Yes – we are unable to undertake the demonstration today.*

– Oh, my goodness! Why?

– *Leaves on the line.*

25

He Disnae Ken

– So, how are the old gang? Still together, I hear?

– *Oh, yes – we're a close-knit group.*

– As you have been for nearly a hundred years!

– *Is it that long? I suppose it must be. Time flies when you don't age.*

– I can imagine. So, can I ask you about some of your colleagues – co-stars, if I may say?

– *Sure.*

– Minnie, now. I've always wondered, is she your sister or girlfriend, or what? There seems to be a lot going on between you, if you know what I mean.

– *Er...mmm. I'd rather not talk about that.*

– And your pal, Don. I understand he's been seeing quite a lot of Minnie lately.

– *Bastard!*

– So, er, have I touched on a sensitive issue?

– *It's up to them.*

– But, how do you feel about it?

– *90 years – 90 fucking years, and she treats me like this!*

– Sorry – I won't press you on that.

– *OK.*

– Moving on, then, how's Pluto?

– *Oh, at least he's still loyal.*

– That's good. That's a nice characteristic of dogs.

– *Oh, yes. Not always of fucking mice, though!*

– Mmm. Anyway, er, what about another of your old colleagues – Goofy? By the way, what kind of animal is he?

– *Fuck knows!*

26

Not the Stork, Then?

– May I offer you my humble thanks for permitting me to carry out this interview, ma'am.

– *We are pleased to take this opportunity to address our people.*

– May I begin by asking about your early life?

– *Please do.*

– I understand that you led an unusually sheltered existence until you were eighteen years old.

– *Absolutely so.*

– Your experience of life was, I assume, very minimal at that time.

– *It was, but, thankfully, my marriage to my dear, late Albert changed all that.*

– I imagine so.

– *We were both very young, of course.*

– Of course, and you had both been brought up in very sheltered environments.

– *We certainly had.*

– But, together, you won the hearts of the nation, if I may say so, ma'am.

– *One would like to think so.*

– And this love and respect, likewise, has been extended to your nine wonderful children.

– *We thank God for extending his blessings to our family.*

– Indeed. Sadly, you might have extended your splendid family even further, if it had not been for the tragic early decease of your beloved Prince Albert.

– *One considered it, but one thought that it would have been inappropriate and unkind to give birth to a child without a father.*

– Er, I don't quite follow you.

– *Well, one decided that one would exercise restraint, to prevent any further pregnancy.*

– Oh?

– *Yes, from that day to this, I have never touched a single bowl of porridge.*

27

Hobbies

– Well, Leo, good to meet you.

– *Likewise.*

– So, what a career, eh?

– *Yes, I suppose so.*

– Oh, you're too modest. Can we talk about some of your achievements?

– *Certainly.*

– Well, first of all, as an inventor, you have become renowned.

– *So it seems.*

– For example, you designed a helicopter 500 years before a practical model was produced.

– *Mmm.*

– And, as an incredible draftsman, you produced some wonderful technical drawings and maps, far ahead of their time.

– *Yes, that was another of my interests.*

– Not to mention that you were a leading botanist in your time.

– *So it appears.*

– And, as a scientist, you were centuries ahead of your peers.

– *Yes, as it has turned out.*

– Notably in the fields of optics and geology.

– *Yes, I was very interested in those areas of study.*

– And, there is still evidence that you were an outstanding architect and sculptor.

– *Ah, yes.*

– Your anatomical studies, too, were outstanding.

– *Thank you.*

– An incredibly busy life, if I may say so.

– *I suppose it was.*

– No time for leisure, eh? Ha ha!

– *Oh, I don't know – I used to do a bit of painting in my spare time.*

– Really?

– *Yes – I knocked up a picture of the Last Supper, one weekend.*

– Oh?

– *And I did a quickie of my girlfriend, Mona.*

28

King of the Ring

– So, Bugsy King – your boxing career really seems to be taking off.

– *Yer.*

– Five wins, five knockouts so far.

– *Yer, that's right.*

– So, what are your ambitions?

– *I want to be a contender. I know I'm good enough.*

– Well, your record so far suggests that could be on the cards.

– *Wot cards?*

– I mean, it could happen.

– *Yer.*

– And, I believe, boxing runs in your family.

– *Oh, yer. Me uncle, Neville King and me dad, Sid King, always had the same boxing style.*

– So I understand, from old films.

– *Yer.*

– So, what would you say is the particular strength of your style?

– *Well, they say we've all got a divine right.*

29

Knock for Knock

– Well, Mr Berg, we've received your accident claim form, but there are just a couple of points we'd like to clear up.

– *OK.*

– So, tell me in your own words what happened.

– *I wish I knew. I was practically stationary, as usual.*

– Go on...

– *It was a lovely night – not a cloud in the sky. The stars were beautiful.*

– So, the visibility was excellent?

– *Oh, yes.*

– Well, then, did you see it coming?

– *Of course, but I couldn't get out of the way.*

– With hindsight, was there anything you could have done to avoid it?

– *Nothing – even when I was sure it would hit me. I'm not a fast mover.*

– We've noticed.

– *Just go with the flow, that's me.*

– So, what happened when the collision occurred?

– *Well, I sustained a lot of damage.*

– So you've reported.

– *Yes – I got an appalling scratch all down one side. I hope they're covered – irresponsible bastards.*

– Fortunately, they are fully insured.

– *Good – the damage was titanic.*

30

He Yis What He Yis

– Sob!

– *You OK, Bluto?*

– No!

– *Come on – talk to me.*

– I don't want to (sob!)

– *Here's a tissue.*

– Thank you.

– *Now, how about telling me about it?*

– Oh, if I have to – but it won't do any good.

– *Come on – get it off your chest.*

– Well...it's him.

– *Who?*

– Oh, you know who - that sailorman.

– *Oh, dear – what about him?*

– It's not really his fault, I suppose.

– *So, what is it?*

– They always make him win!

– *Ah. I see.*

– Everyone thinks I'm a bully and a loser!

– *Well, yes.*

– You see – you're just the same as the rest of them! (sob!)

– *I'm sorry. Tell me about it.*

– Oh, all right.

– *Here – have another tissue.*

– Thanks (sigh), well, you've seen the films.

– *Yes, of course.*

– And I'm always made out to be the baddie!

– *Yes – that's true, but aren't you?*

– No! I'm really not!

– *But aren't you always trying to assault her and beat him up?*

– That's just it – they make me do all that and don't let me show my real self.

– *What do you mean?*

– Well, for instance, I help out at an orphanage in my spare time, I love cooking and I used to do ballet until I got too big.

– *And what about your relationship with Olive?*

– I love her! I love her!

31

Madame

– Oh, they've all been through my hands.

– *I'm sure, Madame.*

– Yes, the finest lords, and ladies, too.

– *So I understand.*

– And I pride myself on never having had any complaints.

– *I'm sure that's true. But I understand today is going to be the culmination of your career.*

– I'd like to think so.

– *And your latest will be here in a few minutes. Are you in form?*

– Oh, yes, I'm feeling really sharp.

– *Good. It's better that way.*

– Of course.

– *So, who's it to be?*

– A couple, this time.

– *Oh – anyone special?*

– Absolutely – I think they're called Louis and Marie.

32

Merry

– So, I think you know why I called you three here today.

– *Yeh, your Maj. So, we've been putting a few ideas together.*

– I knew I could rely on you. I'm running a bit low on cash so I need to kick off a few new – er – let's say projects – I hate the word 'fiddles'.

– *You've come to the right people, guv'nor.*

– I knew I had. So, have you come up with any ideas?

– *We have – and I think you'll like them.*

– Tell me more.

– *Well, your people are walking all over the place for free, wearing out the pavements and impeding the traffic every time they cross the road.*

– Go on.

– *We reckon it's reasonable to implement a pedestrian charge – say, a pound a mile.*

– I think I like it. How would we collect?

– *Fit all of your subjects with a pedometer (at their own cost, of course) which has to be read at the local tax office once a month for the tax to be collected.*

– Excellent – I'll call the Chancellor this afternoon to start making plans.

– *Glad you like it.*

– So, what's next?

– *Al's come up with a doozy.*

– I'm all ears.

– *Here's how it works: we call it VAT – Vehicle Access Tax. You want to reduce noise pollution, don't you?*

– I suppose so.

– *So, let's put a sensor on every car door. If it detects more than ten decibels when the door is slammed, it sends a radio message back to the tax office. Profit on the compulsory sale of the sensors alone should be pretty tidy.*

– Do it.

– *We've got the manufacturers standing by.*

– Any other ideas?

– *I think you'll love this one.*

– Do tell.

– *Well, who owns the air in this kingdom?*

– Say no more. I'll talk to the Chancellor.

– *OK, guv.*

– Right, if that's it, here's your usual wad. Now, piss off, all of you, and on your way out, tell my butler to bring me my pipe and a bowl of baccy. Oh, and a bottle of vodka – I'm feeling like getting merry.

33

Mistaken Identity

– So, George Foreman – so pleased to meet you.

– *My pleasure.*

– Well, I've been reading up on your distinguished career. It's not only been highly successful, but also very varied.

– *You're right there.*

– Heavyweight boxer – twice world champion.

– *Yes.*

– In many people's view, one of the greatest ever.

– *Well, I don't know about that, but I've had a lot of success, yes.*

– You're too modest, George.

– *Ha! Ha!*

– And a minister of the church at one time, I understand.

– *Yes, I did have that privilege.*

– You see! I've been doing my homework.

– *I can tell.*

– And I understand you're a published author, too. You have been busy!

– *I guess I have.*

– Not to mention the grill you invented. I've got one at home, of course, like millions of others.

– *Really? That's great.*

– But there's another career I'd like to ask you about.

– *Sure.*

– Obviously, in your younger days, you were brought up in Lancashire.

– *Er, where's that?*

– Oh, haha, you're being coy!

– *Er...*

– Come on – you were a top star of British cinema.

– *Well, er...*

– Everyone used to look forward to the new George Foreman comedy. So where did you learn to play the ukulele?

34

Mummy's Little Helper

– Well, Mr Carter, I'm sure I'm not the first to congratulate you on this historic discovery.

– *Thank you.*

– And this must have consolidated your reputation as a leader in your profession.

– *That has been my lifelong ambition, as an archaeologist.*

– And, I understand this was not an easy excavation.

– *True – at the last, we had to break through a three-foot-thick stone wall to gain entry to the tomb.*

– It must have been very demanding.

– *It certainly was, but we were determined.*

– Yes – the builders of the tomb were clearly determined to prevent anyone from ever breaking through.

– *That is clear!*

– So, in summary, what did you discover among the grave goods?

– *Well, there was a huge array of objects, all created by the finest craftsmen to accompany Tutankhamun into the after-life.*

– Such as?

– *Well, there were gold chariots, elaborate ceramic vessels, exquisite carvings, inlaid furniture, hundreds of items of jewellery – more than 5,000 objects in all.*

– Fascinating – and all intended by the priests to accompany Tutankhamun into the eternal afterlife.

– *Yes.*

– And, over a period of ten years, your team will be removing everything except the coffin itself?

– *We will.*

– Fascinating – we look forward to hearing about all the treasures.

– *We will be making them available to the museums.*

– Wonderful. So, what is your latest project?

– *Well, we have spent the last six months making entry to the tomb of King Sputum III.*

– Ah – and what is the latest news on the dig?

– *Sadly, we found that the tomb had been desecrated and robbed.*

– Oh, dear.

– *Yes – some thieving ancient Egyptian bastards had nicked it all before we could.*

35

No Bull

– Yes, I've got to say, I'm totally confident.

– *Well, I do understand you've done a lot of preparation for this event.*

– Absolutely – good grub, plenty of exercise with the lads. Yes – I'm in top form.

– *Well, I can see that – you're looking good!*

– Thanks.

– *So, is this your first time?*

– Absolutely, but I've had a good look around the place, of course.

– *Any thoughts about tactics, then?*

– Oh, basically, my main technique will be the charge and the toss. No problem.

– *So, what about your opponents?*

– You're having a laugh! Have you seen them?

– *What do you mean?*

– The sparkly skin-tight suits, the slippers, the dopey hats?

– *Er, yes.*

– Poofters, the lot of them. If I can't thrash them, I'm a heifer!

36

I Love it Here

– So, may I be the latest to congratulate you on being named a saint, even though posthumously.

– *Thank you and God bless you.*

– And, even nearly 2,000 years later, your name is incredibly well-known throughout the world as the patron saint of love.

– *Yes – most gratifying.*

– I understand that, back in the day, you made your name by saving many Christians from persecution.

– *That was my joy.*

– - and that, as a priest, you led a life of the greatest simplicity and poverty.

– *Unfortunately, yes.*

– What makes you say that?

– *Well, let's be frank – we all like a few luxuries in life.*

– Er, yes, I suppose so.

– *And after death, eh? Why not? We're all human.*

– Well, er, yes.

– *But, at least, now, I can afford some of the pleasures of life – or death – haha!*

– Er, I see. So how are you able to achieve that?

– *Well, I've at last got a decent bit of cash coming in each year.*

– Oh, really – how come?

– *Well, I've got a lot of stocks and shares, so, at least every Spring, I get some nice dividends.*

– I see – in what sort of companies?

– *Oh – mostly greetings card firms and florists.*

37

No Copyright

– Where are we now, for fuck's sake?

– *I think we're just coming up to a place called Maidstone.*

– Where is that?

– *In Kent, I think.*

– I guessed that, but how much further is it to Canterbury?

– *I don't know. That guy in the helmet seems to be in charge, but he's too much up his own arse to talk to us lot.*

– I wish I'd rented a fucking horse, like him. This walking is playing hell with my feet. Between you and me, the next time we pass a cart going back to London, I'm thinking of thumbing a lift – stuff Becket!

– *I'm starting to think the same thing! If it wasn't for my boss.*

– And the rest of this lot – what a bunch of oddballs!

– *You're right. My guv'nor is OK, but she's a bit straitlaced.*

– Well, she is a bloody nun.

– *I know, but it means I have to hold back a bit when it's my turn to tell a story.*

– That miller didn't hold back, though – I laughed my hose off at his tale!

– *So did I, mate.*

– Ha ha! But whose idea was it, anyway – all this storytelling? This trip is hard enough anyway, without everyone having to come up with some sort of tale.

– *You're right. I'm not sure who suggested it.*

– Do you know, I think it may have been that funny little geezer with the white beard, wearing a black smock.

– *Oh – I see him. Haven't heard him coming up with a story, though.*

– No, he's keeping quiet, but have you noticed – he's taking notes all the time?

– *Now you mention it – yes.*

– What do you think he's writing about?

– *He's writing down everyone's story.*

– What for?

– *Who knows. Coffee table thing, I imagine,*

– Possibly – making money out of us lot?

– *I doubt it. Anyway, who's going to care, 600 years from now?*

38

Not a good Start

– So, you want to know what really happened?

– *If you don't mind.*

– Well. I suppose it's all going to come out, sooner or later.

– *You're right - so let's start from the beginning.*

– Well, I have to say, the garden was lovely.

– *I can imagine. Go on.*

– Well, of course, I knew the couple – they both seemed very happy there.

– *So, what went wrong?*

– Well, it was her.

– *I see.*

– It started with the tree.

– *I think I've heard about that.*

– Granny Smiths, I think.

– *So, what happened?*

– Oh, I didn't particularly fancy it. I prefer meat. So did she - with me, if you catch my drift.

– *Oh, I see. So, what happened?*

– Well, as I said, it was her. Not to make a thing of it, she came on to me.

– *Oh?*

– Well, I am 8ft long and 3 inches thick.

– *So, er...*

– Adam wasn't interested.

– *You mean?*

– Nine-bob-note job, if you know what I mean.

– *Oh. I see.*

– So, she was totally up for it, given my size and shape.

– *I can imagine.*

– But, of course, I'm more into female snakes, although, admittedly, there weren't too many about at that time.

– *I can imagine.*

– So, cut a long story short, we got it on.

– *OK.*

– Well, God got the hump.

– *I see.*

– He wanted babies – a human race, and all that.

– *So that didn't fit with his plans?*

– Exactly – so he slung them both out.

– *Makes sense.*

39

On the Run

– So, since the accident, I understand most of the animals have now been recaptured.

– *Yes – it hasn't been easy but, thank goodness, there have been no major injuries or losses.*

– That's good to know, but I understand there are a few animals still at liberty.

– *That's right, and we are asking the public to be on the lookout for them.*

– So, how many of the zoo's stock are still free?

– *Four.*

– Are any of them dangerous?

– *Not really, although a couple of them may appear to be.*

– What are they?

– *There's a bear and a tiger, but we are asking the public not to panic.*

– I see, and the others?

– *Just a donkey and a small pig.*

– Well, let's hope that they are soon spotted. It's been a few weeks, now, hasn't it?

– *Yes, but we're confident that we're close to finding them.*

– Oh?

– *Yes – our lead investigator, Christopher Robin, has narrowed down the search. We now believe they are in the Hundred Acre Wood, although we haven't had any communication from him for a while.*

– So, would you advise people locally to keep clear of the danger?

– *Not particularly – they're all a bunch of halfwits, especially the bear; and he's gay, too.*

40

Penitence?

– So, Count, how are you finding it, here in purgatory?

– *Well, it's not heavenly, is it?*

– Right, but you must admit it could have been worse if you hadn't said sorry at the end.

– *I suppose so.*

– At least, you must have convinced the Old Man that you were penitent.

– *Oh, yes – so it seems, thank, er, goodness.*

– And there's some company here to keep you on the straight and narrow.

– *Mmm...*

– And you must admit you were sent here to repent your evil ways.

– *I know, I know, and I'm working on it.*

– Going to the classes?

– *Regularly.*

– Benefiting from the counselling they give here?

– *Oh, er, I think so.*

– And I understand you've made a couple of chums since you've been here. That must help your efforts to redeem yourself.

– *Oh, er, it does, it does.*

– Anyone I may have heard of?

– *Er, maybe.*

– So, who are they?

– *Well, there's Attila, Jack, Adolf and good old Vlad the I.*

41

Pies

– Good day at the fair?

– *Fair.*

– Yeh – go on. I mean, did you sell all your pies?

– *Yeh. Met that bloody kid again on the way there, though.*

– Oh, yes.

– *Wanted to know what I was selling, as if a gross of pies on my bloody head wasn't a clue.*

– I know – I've seen you. So, what did you say?

– *I just said, "What do you think?"*

– Yeh.

– *So he says, "Let's have one".*

– So, what did you say?

– *I said, "Well, give us a penny".*

– Did he?

– *Well, you know the kid – he didn't have any money.*

– So, what happened?

– *He kicked me in the bollocks and pinched five pies.*

42

Grey Skies

– You may kiss my hand.

– *Your Majesty.*

– You may rise.

– *May I offer you my warmest congratulations and God's blessings.*

– We thank you.

– *Long may you reign.*

– I intend so.

– *Are there any tidings of Mary's movements, your Majesty?*

– Mary who?

– *I refer to the pretender, ma'am.*

– Oh, her. I believe she is somewhere in the provinces.

– *On her way to London, I understand.*

– That is of no interest to us.

– *Of course, Majesty. May I enquire as to your plans for the nation under your excellent guardianship?*

– I intend to make England even greater, as it was under my honoured forefather, King Hal.

– *May God bless your ambitions, ma'am.*

– I foresee a long and glorious reign for myself.

– *There can be no doubt of that, Majesty.*

– At the age of 17, I foresee a reign of more than half a century, taking us well into the seventeenth century.

– *I look forward to serving you throughout your, no doubt, noble reign, ma'am.*

– Keep your nose clean, and you shall.

– *I must confess myself impressed by the authority with which, as a person of modest years, you have already seized the reins of this great nation.*

– I thank you for your loyalty, milord.

– *In a matter of a mere nine days, you have already established your authority over your kingdom and earned the love of your people.*

– One does ones best.

– KNOCK...KNOCK

– Who is this that enters without one's permission?

– *They look like the palace guards, ma'am.*

– They have their swords drawn!

– *Er, I'm just going to the toilet.*

43

Prêt à Manger

– You been out in the stable lately, Abe?

– *What, in this weather? It's bloody freezing out there, Mir!*

– Tell me about it! So, you haven't seen them, then.

– *Who?*

– The couple squatting there.

– *What couple?*

– Remember that pair that turned up this morning, wanting a room? I think they were here for the census. I had to turn them away.

– *I must have been indoors, mending my sandals. Who were they, anyway?*

– That's just it. I've got no idea who the fuck they are!

– *So, what about them?*

– I've just been out there, and they're sitting on the ground in the stable, making themselves at home. They've got a flask of tea and a bloody picnic.

– *Cheeky bastards! They're not disturbing the animals, are they?*

– Jennie and Thor? No, they're fine. But that's not the worst of it.

– *So what's the other problem then?*

– She's only fucking dropped?

– *Dropped? Dropped what?*

– A baby! She's had a fucking baby in our barn!

– *You're having a laugh!*

– Go out and have a look!

– *I will.*

EXIT

RE-ENTERS

– *For fuck's sake!*

– What?

– *You've got to come and see this*

– What?

– *There's three weirdos out there in crowns and long embroidered frocks, kneeling down and giving presents to the fucking baby!*

– What sort of presents?

– *Christ knows; pots of something or other. But there's a box too. I caught a glimpse of what's inside and, I've never seen gold, but I'll be fucked if that's not what it was.*

– So they're not as dirt poor as they look!

– *Not now, anyway! And that's not all – I could swear I heard angel voices singing.*

– No!

– *Yes! Who the fuck is Good King Wenceslas, anyway?*

44

Procrastination

– I thought I'd made it completely clear to him from the start.

– *He knew who you were, I suppose?*

– My first words to him.

– *Well, that should have been clear enough.*

– Yes, and I told him exactly how that bastard brother of mine had killed me.

– *I bet that made him mad.*

– You would have thought so.

– *So, what was the problem?*

– You tell me.

– *Maybe it was a case of 'revenge is a dish best served cold'.*

– Cold? It was fucking freezing by the time he got off is arse and did something about it.

– *Well, that wasn't necessarily a bad thing*

– Not in itself, if he hadn't messed around and done a lot of harm in the meantime.

– *What do you mean?*

– Well, for a start, he topped a lovely old boy – a bit of a pain, but he used to give me good advice. Pity he didn't suss my brother – nobody saw that coming.

– *Oh dear! I suppose it was all covered up.*

– Oh, yes – accident, mistake and all that. But it drove the daughter potty – finished up drowning herself.

– *Oh dear!*

– Bloody right – she was a lovely girl. If things had turned out differently, they would probably have got married.

– *Sad.*

– And that's not all. He finished up icing a few of his mates, not to mention my ex-missis – I think you met her the other day – before he finally got round to killing my brother.

– *Bloody hell!*

– Exactly. He always was a lazy little bastard!

45

Revenge

– I've never seen you so worked up, Beaky.

– *You don't know what I've been through, pal.*

– Well, tell me about it.

– *It's that bastard, his Maj.*

– Oh?

– *Well, you haven't seen a lot of my family recently, have you?*

– Now you mention it – no.

– *No – they're gone, mate.*

– Where?

– *Fucking brown bread (well, black, actually).*

– Shit! What happened?

– *It's that arsehole – His Maj.*

– Yeh?

– *"Bake me a nice pie tomorrow", he says to his cook. "Something different. I'm sick of steak and kidney and chicken and mushroom".*

– Oh, so what did he come up with?

– *Fucking blackbird!*

– You're having a laugh!

– *No, so he slings a bloody great net over that tree where we used to roost at night, and next morning he catches a couple of dozen of us. I only got away by the skin of my beak.*

– Shit! What did he do then?

– *Only made them into a fucking pie!*

– The bastard!

– *Served it up that evening. Even made his minstrels play a little blackbird song. No respect.*

– So, there was nothing you could do about it?

– *Not then – but I'll have 'em – the whole lot of 'em.*

– So, what are you planning to do?

– *Return the bloody favour – to the whole household!*

– How?

– *Well, I've started already. One of the maids was in the garden this afternoon, hanging out the washing.*

– So, what did you do?

– *Pecked off her effing nose!*

– No! So, what about the king and queen?

– *Well, I know where to find him – the old bastard spends every afternoon in his counting-house, and she'll be in the parlour, feeding her face.*

– So?

– *I'm going to give a whole new meaning to the phrase 'nose job'.*

46

Robby's Camp

– So, Marian, how are you finding life here in Sherwood?

– *Well, it's OK – at least I've escaped the clutches of the sheriff.*

– So, why did you decide to come here, to the forest?

– *Basically, it was either this or the castle dungeon.*

– Oh?

– *Yes, you see it was the fourth time I'd been arrested for shoplifting in Nottingham market, and I was up for a few months inside.*

– Ah.

– *So, when the Sheriff's officers came to arrest me, I did a runner.*

– Naturally.

– *- and the forest was the obvious place to hide.*

– That makes sense.

– *- and after a day or so, I chanced on Robin's camp.*

– That was lucky.

– *Mmm...*

– So, if you don't mind my asking, is it true that Robin and you, er, got it on?

– *You're joking!*

– Oh?

– *Have you met Robin and the gang?*

– Not yet.

– *Well, let me tell you a bit about them...*

– OK, well, I've heard of Little John...

– *Oh, yes, the only thing little about him is down there – catch my drift?*

– Mmm, I see.

– *And as for the Tryer, as I call him.*

– Tryer?

– *Tryer F... think about it.*

– Oh, I'm with you.

– *Then there's Much, the Miller's son.*

– Yes?

– *Or 'not much' – I'll say no more.*

– Will Scarlet?

– *He prefers pink, actually. With me?*

– Mmm... But, wait a minute – isn't that Robin, coming through the trees?

– *Oh, yes. Hi Robin!*

– Oh, hellay Marian! Mmm, who's your bona new chum?

47

A Distinguished Immigrant

– So, Señor Hiller, I need to ask you a few questions to establish your eligibility for Supplementary Benefit.

– *I understand.*

– I am sure you understand that Argentina is not a wealthy country.

– *Unfortunately, yes.*

– And we need to be very sure of the eligibility of each applicant.

– *Naturally.*

– So, I believe you are an immigrant.

– *I am.*

– And when did you first settle here?

– *Er, in 1945.*

– And your place of birth was?

– *Er, Austria, Austria.*

– Ah, and what was your reason for emigrating here?

– *I was the victim of political prejudice and my position was made redundant.*

– I see. It was a sudden decision, then?

– *Very sudden.*

– And your occupation in your native country?

– *Er, I was a leader.*

– A boy scout leader?

– *Among other things.*

– I see…so what are your plans now that you have settled here in Argentina?

– *Well, I need a role where I can wield immense and unquestioning authority.*

– That may not be immediately possible, I'm afraid.

– *That is unacceptable.*

– I'm sorry?

– *I demand a position where I can exercise my indomitable will and faultless judgement.*

– Er, I'm not sure…

– *But, I am!*

– Well, if you really want a job, I have a Mrs Cohen who is looking for a cleaner…

– *What!*

– Or Mr Greenberg needs a shop assistant.

– *Fuck right off!*

– Listen, if you are not going to let me help you, you can just piss off back to where you came from!

– *I might just do that – but, this time, no more Mr Nicey Nicey!*

48

Santa's Little Helper

– *All right, Rudy*

– Oh, hello, Hornie. Yea, you know - getting there, getting there.

– *Look, I don't want to be inquisitive, but I heard you weren't getting on too well with the herd. Because of your – you know...*

– Yeh. Who wants to play fucking 'lock the antlers', anyway. Fucking stupid game.

– *You're right, I suppose. I'm quite good at it, though, actually.*

– I imagine you are.

– *But things must be looking up a bit now, aren't they. I mean, I heard about what went on at Christmas.*

– Oh, that. Yes.

– *Well, tell me about it. What did actually happen?*

– Well, you remember how foggy it was last Christmas Eve – couldn't see your hoof in front of your face?

– *Yeh – I remember.*

– All right. Well, I was just tucking in to a nice bit of hay, and looking forward to a quiet night when the Old Man comes over. He says, "A word regarding your nose, Rudolf". Well, I assumed he was going to take the piss just like the others. You know what he's like – he loves kids but he's a cunt to everyone else. But he said, "In this weather I think you may be a help to me". I thought, "Here it comes". He says, "Look, with your nose, you're just the one to lead my sleigh tonight". I just said, "Yes, of course, Guv'nor.

Whatever you say." So much for my quiet night.

– *So how was it?*

– Do not ask. A fucking nightmare.

– *But the guys were a bit more respectful to you afterwards, eh?*

– Oh, yes. Crawling bastards. "You'll go down in history, mate!" Sarcastic sods.

– *But they started letting you join in their games, didn't they?*

– Oh, yes. They asked if I fancied a game of hoofball.

– *So did you?*

– You're joking – I told them to go and fuck themselves.

49

Fireworks

– Yes, as the caretaker, I was the one that dealt with the guards.

– *Well, thank goodness they turned up! It could have been a disaster.*

– Tell me about it!

– *Well, you tell me – what went on that day?*

– Well, I went down to the cellar to do my regular inspection – I have a look once a week to check on how my home-made beer is progressing.

– *And what did you find that day?*

– Well, everything looked normal at first…

– *OK.*

– Well, then I saw that bloke, Fawkes.

– *What was he doing?*

– He'd just dropped off another couple of barrels.

– *What was in them?*

– He said it was cement – he told me he was going to be building a house.

– *Didn't you think of checking?*

– He was giving me sixpence a day.

– *I get it.*

– I'm a poor man.

– *So, who called the cops?*

– No idea – it wasn't him or me.

– *Lucky they turned up, then, bearing in mind what they found!*

– Yes – if that lot had gone off, it would have ruined my beer. As it is, I had to spend the rest of the afternoon and evening "helping them with their enquiries", as they say.

– *Ah – a bit of a nuisance.*

– I'll say! I got a hell of a bollocking from the missis when I got home.

– *Oh. Why?*

– Well, it was November the fifth. I'd promised to spend the evening letting off fireworks with the kids.

50

Seasonal Generosity

RING

- Delivery!
- *Hi.*
- Morning, miss – here you are.
- *Wow, thanks – a little tree!*
- Yes, I think it's a pear tree.
- *So it is – how lovely! And there's a big bird on that branch!*
- Yes, it looks like a partridge to me.
- *I'll plant it straight away. Oh, it's from Cyril. How thoughtful of him.*
- Well, I'm off.

– *Bye then.*

RING

– *Oh, hello again.*

– Another delivery for you.

– *Oh, wow!*

– Here you go.

– *How lovely – two doves. He's so romantic.*

– And here you are...

– *Another tree – with another partridge. He's such a silly boy! Bye.*

RING

– *Oh, er, hello.*

– Delivery.

– *Er – what's in that crate?*

– I think it's chickens - hens.

– *Chickens?*

– Yes. Three.

– *Don't tell me.*

– Yes they're from the same address.

– *Er...lovely. Thanks.*

– Just a mo...

– *Oh!*

– Here you are...

– *Two more doves!*

– And, er, this tree.

– *Thanks – I'll plant it with the other one. Perhaps the doves will all nest there with the partridges. So lovely of him, but a bit over the top, perhaps.*

RING

– *Oh. It's you again.*

– Yes. Some more birds. I think they're called colly birds.

– *No! Silly bugger – where does he think I'm going to keep them?*

– Don't ask me. I'll just get the hens.

– *Three more?*

– Er… and the doves and the tree.

– *He's mad! Does he realize what he's doing?*

– Can't help you, darling. Well, bye.

RING

– *No, not you.*

– Here – I think it's rings – five.

– *Well, that's more like it.*

– And, er…

– *No!*

– Sorry, I'm not allowed to take them back.

– *Sob!*

– Mmm…

– *The idiot! Ok – I suppose you'd better bring them in. God knows where I'm going to put everything.*

RING

– *You again.*

– Yep.

– *Are those geese in that crate?*

– I think so.

– *Anything else in the van?*

– I'm afraid so. Just a tree, doves, hens etc. can you give me a hand?

– *The bastard – he's crazy*

– I don't know about that, darling.

– *Listen – I'm not accepting any more deliveries from that arsehole!*

– Well, that's a problem. There's a lot more stuff back at the depot.

– *No! What?*

– Well, there's seven swans, a crowd of drummers, pipers and dancing girls and a team of aristocrats, leaping about like lunatics.

51

Sharesy

– Well, she was a nice kid.

– *So I understand.*

– And I didn't mean to startle her.

– *I'm sure you didn't.*

– I just thought we could hang out together for a bit.

– *Well, that should have been OK, but...*

– Oh, I know – fucking arachnophobia – I hate it.

– *Well, a lot of people suffer from it.*

– Yeh – depressing.

– *And you should have thought about that.*

– Yes, I suppose so, but that was my tuffet, after all.

– *That's beside the point.*

– I know, I know.

– *So, why did you do it?*

– Sharesy.

– *Sharesy?*

– Yes – I do love a bit of curds and whey.

52

Side Job

– Morning, Alf.

– *Oh, hallo Mr McManus.*

– You got the message that I was coming to make a site inspection?

– *Yes. Sorry I wasn't here when you first arrived.*

– No problem. I've had a good look around.

– *Oh, good.*

– Are you happy, yourself, with progress so far?

– *Yes, in general. We're on schedule overall.*

– Good. Most of the work seems to be up to standard.

– *Er...most?*

– Well, I've got one little concern I need to talk to you about.

– *Oh…OK.*

– Yes – it's mostly about the paintwork.

– *Ah, I see.*

– Yes. I have to ask – your painter – where did you find him?

– *Well, as you know, the other one left suddenly. A family emergency, we were told. So, er, what problems did you have with the new guy?*

– Well, just a couple of comments…

– *OK.*

– The steelwork, for example. The protective coat of paint is usually standard red lead.

– *Yes.*

– Er, well, I think I've seen about seven different colours there, and all in odd designs.

– *Mmm, yes, I'd noticed that, but as long as the metal is protected from rust, I've left him alone.*

– But – those weird faces – that must be slowing down his productivity.

– *So far, he's on schedule, so I've left him to it.*

– Mmm, OK.

– *So, you're happy for me to keep him on?*

– Yes – I suppose so, as long as he's getting the job done.

– *OK.*

– By the way – funny little chap. Where did you find him?

– *Oh, we just got chatting at a bus-stop, the day after the other chap suddenly left. He mentioned he was a painter, but he didn't have a lot on at the moment.*

– Oh, I see. What's his name?

– *Oh, Pablo something.*

53

Size Isn't Everything

– Well, big boy, sorry to have to see you up here so soon.

– *Me, too, pal.*

– You were only young, weren't you?

– *29*

– And, as far as I can tell, you were in the pink.

– *Oh, I was.*

– And you had a whole army backing you up.

– *Yeh – you'd have thought so.*

– So, how did it all happen?

– *Well, the bastards pushed me into it. It's happened all my life, since I was a kid at school.*

– I can imagine. I suppose that's only to be expected, though.

– *Yeh, but I never liked it. I just want to be friends with everyone.*

– I can understand that. Who doesn't?

– *Yes – I'm an easygoing guy, really.*

– Well, I can tell that.

– *But, of course, I'm quite well-built – six foot nine (not nine foot, like people say) – so people think I'm tough.*

– That's natural.

– *But all I'm really interested in is my embroidery – oh, and I do like an occasional game of dominoes.*

– Er, who doesn't, eh?

– *But when those bastards challenged us, I got pushed to the front, as usual.*

– So I heard.

– *And that Saul – cowardly bastard – put that kid up for the row.*

– I suppose he knew he was the tribe's open sling champion?

– *Course he did, but I didn't.*

– Yes – how were you to know?

– *Well, it was supposed to be a hands-on fight. I'd have beaten the kid, of course, but I wouldn't have dreamt of hurting him.*

– So, what went wrong?

– *Well, they gave me a sword and a spear, but there was no way I was going to use them.*

– So, what about him?

– *Well, the kid turned up with his Olympic standard sling and a bagful of professional 35gram stones.*

– And?

– *I stepped up, ready to shake hands with the kid.*

– Yeh?

– *Well, we're still 20 feet apart and the little so-and-so lets loose with his sling!*

– Ooh – that must have stung!

– *You bet it did – cheating little Yid bastard!*

54

Square Eyes

– So, Mr Baird, allow me to add my congratulations on your new invention.

– *Thank you – this has been a very special day for me.*

– I can imagine.

– *Yes – the concept is one I first considered some years ago. It has taken many years to bring it to fruition.*

– Of course. Not surprisingly, may I say.

– *Thank you.*

– So, I can imagine this system will have a huge impact on the entertainment and communication industries.

– *That has been my hope.*

– The culmination of a lifetime's work, I gather.

– *You could say that, indeed.*

– And you have, deservedly, received huge international acclaim over the last few days – a busy time for you.

– *Yes, it has been a gratifying, but exhausting couple of days, talking to the press and conducting demonstrations.*

– I can imagine. So, I understand this is the last interview you will be giving for a while.

– *Yes – thank goodness.*

– So – what are your plans now? A nice quiet evening at home?

– *Absolutely.*

– And how will you be relaxing, if I may ask?

– *Oh, nothing special – I expect I'll send out for a pizza and watch some crap on telly.*

55

Don't Brag

– Morning, Hal.

– *Ah, good morning, Lord Inverness. I'd heard you were back at court. It's been a few years, hasn't it?*

– Tell me about it!

– *So, what has kept you away? The old trouble, I suppose?*

– No, that seems to have cleared up a bit. No, it's been a nervous thing. The quacks told me I needed complete rest with no contact with the world, so I've been confined to barracks up there for a few years.

– *Sorry to hear it. So, how's the good Lady Inverness?*

– Oh, Knees-together Nellie? She seems OK. I've got to say, though, that if it hadn't been for a few chambermaids and a couple of nurses over the last few years, I'd have thought it had dropped off.

– *I can imagine.*

– And if I have to play another game of bloody dominoes, I'll throw up bone-marrow!

– *So, what brings you down here to court?*

– I just needed to get away from her and rekindle a few old acquaintances, if you know what I mean.

– *I see.*

– So, how about you. Are you still with the Dago?

– *No. that's all over.*

– You don't surprise me – I've always thought she was a bit too strait-laced for you.

– *Mmm*

– Here's another one you would want to have steered clear of: can't remember her name, Ann, I think, but she'd been brought up in some foreign court. Had that posh French accent and she was so far up her own arse it wasn't funny. Mind you a few of us went up the same place, but I got the impression she'd set her sights a bit higher.

– *Yes, it seems she had.*

– And what about that Janey Seymour – is she still around? Nice childbearing hips, if I remember. I think she'd had a couple of kids up North somewhere, but we had some fun for a couple of months.

– *I haven't seen her for a while. I believe she's passed away.*

– Oh, that's sad. Women, eh? You probably don't remember that Cloggie bird I was seeing in Flanders a few years ago? She'd have suited you. Paper bag job, but I found her very cuddly when I was over there on a business trip.

– *Er, yes – I believe I do recall her.*

– Fun times, eh? And that Ann had a little cousin, didn't she, Catherine something. Used to put herself about like there was no tomorrow, and she was only a teenager. I must say I felt a bit like a cradle snatcher when it was my turn.

– *I can imagine.*

– Oh, and there was Catherine Parr; she was a bit of a goer in her time, if I remember – and I do!

– *You are referring to my present wife, I presume.*

– Oh....er....what....yes....erm.... a true lady. We all respected her, of course.

– *Of course. Well, I must be leaving you now – matters of state, you understand. These gentlemen will look after you.*

– Oh, I wondered what the guards were doing here.

– *Yes, they will be seeing that you get a bit of a stretch in the Tower. I hope you enjoy being quartered there for a while.*

– Hold on! Hold on! What did I do? What did I do? ....

56

Swopsies

– Oh, hi!

– *Hi!*

– Er, Frankie, is it? Frankie Stein?

– *That's me.*

– They told me you were here. It's been a while.

– *You're right - it must be ten years.*

– At least. So, er, you're looking good.

– *Thanks.*

– But, er, to be honest, your face looks a bit familiar, but I don't think I'd have recognised you.

– *Well, people change, you know.*

– Yes, of course. So, how, er, have you had some work done, if you know what I mean?

– *Er, kind of. Why?*

– Well, let's be frank, you were no oil painting last time I saw you.

– *Don't worry – no need to beat about the bush. We've known each other long enough.*

– True. Well, come on – after that accident, your face was pretty well buggered up, wasn't it?

– *It was. Those were a very embarrassing few years, but I had to keep working – the project I was working on was too revolutionary.*

– So I hear.

– *And, among the body parts I managed to assemble was someone killed in a bad car accident, who had donated his body to science.*

– I thought I recognized that face. George Clooney, isn't it?

57

Technology

– Morning, Ug.

– *Morning, Grunt.*

– Busy?

– *Not really. Killed a mammoth last week, so the tribe's OK for grub for a month or so, even if it gets a bit high.*

– That's nice. Time for a bit of rest, eh?

– *Yeh, so I'm doing a bit of work on my engineering project.*

– Oh, I heard about that. How's it progressing?

– *Slow, if I'm honest.*

– Oh, I'm sorry to hear that

– *Yeh – but I'm not giving up.*

– So, what seems to be the problem?

– *Well, it's a technical issue.*

– Oh?

– *Yes – the body of the thing's coming along nicely.*

– That's good.

– *Yes – I reckon it would hold a whole aurochs joint – you know how heavy they are.*

– Tell me about it – the last time I killed one I had to cut it up into steaks on-site and get all the kids to carry them home.

– *I know – you can wear out a couple of flints like that, too.*

– I did.

– *Yes - so I know there's a market for my product, as long as I can iron out a couple of technical issues.*

– So, what seems to be the biggest hurdle?

– *The wheels.*

– Oh, OK.

– *Yes – I've tried square, triangular and oval, but they don't seem to give me the performance I want.*

– Hmm. How about round?

– *Oh, I don't think that would work.*

58

Thanks, Gran.

– I must say, Ridey, your gran kept this house in good nick.

– *Of course she did, with all those millions grandad left her.*

– How old was she, actually?

– *Oh, about 57, I think.*

– No age, eh? Ha ha!

– *No. She could have gone on for years, the old bitch. Anyway, pass the champagne and plump my pillows up a bit, love.*

– There you go. I've always thought this would be a wonderfully comfortable bed.

– *I know. I believe it cost her a fortune.*

– So, everything went perfectly to plan, eh?

– *Couldn't have gone better – my scheme was brilliant, though I say it myself.*

– And they'll never find the body – the idiots.

– *How did you persuade Wolfie to do it in the end?*

– Oh, we go back a long way. We had a private arrangement – he would always let me have a nice leg of mutton or pork from time to time, but you know what a greedy bastard he was, and lazy with it.

– *I know – you told me he's even been too lazy to chase after sheep, lately.*

– Yes – all he used to do was raid the odd chicken coop – and then he'd always complain he got a mouthful of feathers, so when I offered him a nice chubby old lady, that he would hardly have to get out of bed for, and would feed him for a week, he jumped at it.

– *I told you he would, the idiot, and it wasn't hard to persuade gran to take a constitutional in the woods.*

– Then, once he had finished her off, bones and all, I finished him off. He didn't even see the axe coming.

– *Twit.*

– Yes – you were right about that, too.

– *So, when we've finished 'mourning' and I'm officially named the heir, what's the first thing we'll do?*

– Well, I was thinking - to start with, a nice flat in Marbella, a couple of new cars and...

– *I love you, Woody. Come here!*

59

That's The Way to Do It

– So, Toby – tell me about it.

– *They were a fucking nightmare, the pair of them.*

– I can imagine.

– *And it wasn't all him, you know.*

– Oh?

– *She would wind him up like there was no tomorrow when nobody else was around. "Big Nose", "Schnozzle". All of that.*

– I can imagine what that would do to an aggressive guy like him.

– *You've gotta believe it – of course, he retaliated, big time – you've seen that club of his.*

– Oh, yes - and when she called the police, what happened?

– *Well, for a start, he iced the copper – then he went on one of his fucking rampages.*

– So I understand.

– *Even ran into a circus and had a row with a clown – killed him too.*

– Yes.

– *Well, that's when they finally managed to get him under arrest.*

– So I hear – thank goodness...Well, now the hangman's going to put a permanent end to it all tomorrow morning at the jail.

– *I know.*

– But I understand there's three things the police are still baffled by.

– *Oh?*

– Yes – for one, why did he never hurt you?

– *And?*

– Where did he get his drugs from.

– *Mmm…*

– And why do they call you Dealer Dog Toby?

60

The 23rd Farm

- *Hello Sheila. How are things, darling?*
- Hi Shirl. Oh, pretty good, actually.
- *Tell me - how's that Shepherd treating you these days?*
- Oh – he's lovely. You couldn't want any better. No wonder they call him the Lord.

– *Hmm. So I've heard.*

– It's true – he's an absolute sweetie. He always manages to find us a nice bit of grass – especially by that lake – it's so quiet there.

– *Well, that's nice, but I must say he worries me a bit.*

– But he's sweet. Oh, he's a bit self-righteous, but he keeps us girls on the straight and narrow, including that Shona – you know what she's like. And have you seen that bloody great rod of his?

– *Er, as a matter of fact – no. I can imagine that... oh, sorry, you mean his shepherd's staff.*

– Yes. If he says, "Get in that pen, for fuck's sake!" ('scuse me) you do it.

– *I can imagine. But something still tells me he's a bit phoney – all this lovey-dovey stuff about looking after us forever. And by the way, where is Shona – I haven't seen her for a couple of days.*

– Nor have I, I'm pleased to say – the little bitch. But you're too cynical. Look, you know that wadi that's full of wolves – 'The

Valley of Death', they call it – it used to frighten the fleece off me in there, but when he's with us, I feel a lot better – as long as he's carrying that staff of his. He even stops there for us to have a bit of a nibble.

– *Nice of him I'm sure, but I'd keep an eye on him. There's something he's not telling us.*

– Oh, don't be silly. By the way, I meant to ask, what's that stuff they anoint us with?

– *I think they call it 'sheep dip'.*

– Oh, right. He's pretty generous with it, anyway. Tastes funny, though.

– *Hmm.*

– Well, anyway, as far I can see, things are looking good for the rest of my life, now. He's got a nice dry barn, too.

– *Well, good for you, darling. Where is he now, by the way?*

– Oh, he's gone home for his tea.

– *Nice. What's he having?*

– Something called 'mutton chops', I think.

61

Death of a Pharaoh

– May I respectfully bid you welcome to Gizeh, great Pharaoh.

– *You may rise, Abdul.*

– Permit me to aid you to descend from your litter.

– *Yes, you may crouch.*

– It will be my honour, highness.

– *It will.*

– Before drawing aside the curtain to your pavilion, great one, that you may gaze upon your construction, may I remind you of the statistics relating to the creation of your Great Pyramid, a task to the supervision of which I have had the privilege of dedicating myself for the greater part of my adult life?

– *Continue, Vizier.*

– Well, your magnificence, the construction has taken thirty years. It uses nine million stones, each weighing twelve tons; they were brought from the Upper Nile, two thousand five hundred miles away, on a fleet of 8,000 barges; five thousand slaves worked day and night on the project, of whom six hundred died each year in on-site accidents. The pyramid is the tallest man-made structure in the known world and will be so, our priests predict, for the next three thousand years.

– *I see.*

– So, may I now command your slaves to draw back the drapes, that you may gaze upon the great structure, your Magnificence?

– *You may.*

– ...

– So, my Pharaoh, does it meet with your approval?

– *Not really – it's a bit fucking boring. Knock it down.*

– You cunt!!

62

Happy Ever After

– I'm so happy, Charms!

– *So am I, Cinders!*

– It's been a fairytale, hasn't it?

– *It certainly has, darling.*

– And the great thing is that everybody has won.

– *Yes, we're not the only happy ones.*

– That's right. I talked to my fairy godmother only this morning.

– *Oh. How is she?*

– She's doing great – her magic business has really taken off since word got around about the ball.

– *That's wonderful!*

– She's doing three shows a week and, guess what! She's been offered a TV series.

– *Wow! I'll look forward to seeing that. And by the way, how's your dad?*

– Well, he's written a book about the whole thing. It's in the best sellers list already.

– *That's great.*

– And guess what! They're adapting it for the stage - it's called a panto, I think – it'll be on by Christmas.

– *Wonderful! And how about your father's page – Butter/Butley?*

– Buttons? Oh, he's been given a part in the panto – playing himself, and he's got a gig on the circuit doing standup. He's a laugh!

– *And Horace and Gavin?*

– They're getting married next month.

63

Do Tell

– He was always a bloody nuisance, ever since he was a little kid.

– *So I've heard.*

– His mother and I were always having to go up to the school after he'd been caught nicking stuff or fighting.

– *Oh, dear.*

– Yes – he's been a complete nightmare for years. I don't know where he gets it from.

– *That must have been a constant worry.*

– Tell me about it! Don't forget – I've got an image to keep up.

– *Haha – er, mmm.*

– We talked to his teachers – even got him some counselling, but he finished up punching the psychiatrist, so she refused to see him again.

– *Ah!*

– You finish up just not loving 'em, and the neighbours were always up in arms, too – vandalism and aggressiveness.

– *So, what did you do?*

– What could we do? The wife and I just wanted to get him off our hands.

– *I can imagine.*

– And when he started beating his mum up – that was the last straw!

– *No! really?*

– Yeh – but it was Gessler who gave me the opportunity.

– *To do what?*

– To ice the little bastard before he could do any more harm.

– *So, what happened?*

– Gessler had me arrested for some bloody ongoing problem. He said, “So, Tell, I hear you’re something of a marksman with the crossbow.” I said, “I like to think so”.

– *Oh.*

– So he says, “I’ve arrested your boy here, too. If you can shoot an apple off the top of his head, I’ll let you both go”.

– *So, what did you say?*

– I thought – here’s my chance to get rid of the problem and blame Gessler.

– *So, did you?*

– No – I fucking missed and hit the apple. Anyway, he was arrested two weeks later for armed robbery. He’s doing 30 years now - the little bastard.

64

The Real Hero

– Nice to see you back in London, mate.

– *Thanks – good to be here, I must say, though if it hadn't been for those Bow bells I'd have left and gone back home ages ago.*

– Well, you've certainly seen some adventures over the last couple of years.

– *You can say that again!*

– I heard you were in North Africa.

– *That's right – Morocco.*

– So, how did you come to be there?

– *Long story. Worked my passage by helping them out with a rodent problem.*

– Yeh?

– *Yes. Morocco's a dump, by the way, but I managed to get to meet the Sultan.*

– Wow! So how did that go?

– *Well, as it would happen, they had a major rat infestation at the time, and I was able to clear it up for them.*

– That's impressive. I bet they were grateful.

– *Very.*

– So, er, did the old Sultan reward you at all?

– *Nah! A couple of bowls of cream and all the rats I could eat.*

– Sounds OK.

– *Yeh. That wanker I was with, Dick, didn't do a thing, but they gave him a fucking chest-full of gold.*

– That's life for you.

– *Yeh. Well, see you later, Tibbles.*

65

The Seven 21st Century Virtues

Modern life is characterized by a number of personal qualities and behaviours which are widely encouraged as positive goals and activities to which we should all aspire. Here are some of them:

1. It is admirable to strive, as successful people do, to better yourself and become financially prosperous, creating wealth and status for yourself.

   (Avarice?)

2. You are encouraged, through the media, to acquire and enjoy all the luxuries that 21st

Century life can offer; look at the ads for good food, drink and indulgences!

(Gluttony?)

3. It is healthy to take it easy – find ways of relaxing and enjoying your leisure time. Use labour-saving devices and chill out.

(Sloth?)

4. Anger, at the wrongs of the world or even directed at oneself for one's own misfortunes or failures is a forgivable attitude. Indeed, the most extreme expression of this attitude is named as suicide, which is, by the way, becoming legal in an increasing number of countries.

(Wrath?)

5. Our attention is constantly drawn to successful or wealthy people in various fields – people whose lavish lifestyles we cannot hope to emulate, but which we are implicitly encouraged to wish we could.

(Envy?)

6. We are warmly encouraged to enjoy the pleasures of the flesh. Magazine articles advise on improving the quality of our sexual encounters, and we are encouraged to admire or be amused by those celebrities who indulge in multiple partnerships.

(Lust?)

7. Believe in yourself, have confidence, you can be greater than anyone else – be a winner! Exercise your full potential and rise above the crowd. You're worth it!

(Pride?)

Who's right – or have things changed so much?

66

The Wanderer

– All right. Have a seat, grandad.

– *Take these cuffs off!*

– Not just yet.

– *What am I doing here – I never done nuffink.*

– So you say, but my constable's not so sure.

– *'E never saw me do nuffink!*

– Well, let's talk about it.

– *There's nuffink to talk about.*

– Well, I think, maybe, there is. What were you doing in Lady Witherspoon's bedroom tonight, anyway?

– *I was just having a look around. Nuffink wrong with that, is there?*

– Well, maybe there is. Constable Gander wouldn't have arrested you otherwise.

– *There was no need – I wasn't pinching nuffink!*

– (Sigh). How many times has this happened, Jim?

– *Two or three, maybe.*

– No, Jim, this is the eleventh time we've had to arrest you for housebreaking. It's got to stop, old man.

– *I can't help it if I'm interested in inferior design.*

– Interior.

– *I fought it looked quite nice.*

– Ahhh. That's beside the point. It's a lot more serious this time, isn't it?

– *You mean them pearls? They was only paste.*

– That, yes, but, then, there's Lord Witherspoon.

– *I didn't mean to 'urt 'im. There was no need for 'im to get aggressive. I didn't do 'im any 'arm.*

– You threw Lord Witherspoon down the bloody stairs!

– *'E tripped.*

– That's not what he says, and I'm inclined to believe him. He's got some nasty bruises, especially on his left leg – he's had to go to hospital. He's not a young man, you know.

– *It's 'is own fault.*

– What do you mean?

– *'E wouldn't say 'is prayers.*

– Oh, dear.

67

Ambition

– So, Mr Twist, tell me a little bit about yourself.

– *Well, councillor, I live in the East End.*

– How long have you been there?

– *All my life, of course, since I was born in 1790, like my dad and my grandad, going back hundreds of years, I think.*

– Do you like it there?

– *Of course not, but I can't move.*

– Why not?

– *I couldn't go on the lag with my whole family – we'd starve.*

– I see, so, what do you do for a living?

– *I'm a general labourer.*

– How much do you earn each week?

– *Eight or ten shillings, when I can find work.*

– How often is that?

– *About nine months a year, I suppose.*

– How many children have you got?

– *Four. Two more died as babies, and I lost my eldest son.*

– When you have no work, how do you pay your rent and buy food?

– *The little ones make about sixpence a day, sweeping crossings and my wife makes matchboxes. They pay her threepence per gross. Some days we don't eat, of course. The littlest one, Oliver, is only three, so it'll be a year or two before he can go out to work.*

– When you have work, how many hours do you do each day?

– *12-14.*

– How many people live in your house?

– *My family and three other families.*

– On another topic, what party do you vote for?

– *I'm not allowed to vote, am I?*

– Are your family all healthy?

– *Not really – same as all of our neighbours in East London, we don't get a lot to eat and, anyway, we couldn't afford to see a doctor.*

– Any problems with the law?

– *Well, one of my sons once stole a loaf of bread.*

– What happened to him?

– *Well, he was hanged, of course.*

– So, what brings you to us today?

– *I don't want us all to go to the workhouse. I've heard stories.*

– I'm afraid that is sometimes inevitable, for example, if you can't pay your rent.

– *That's why I've come to see you today – to try to get your help.*

– Oh?

– *I was wondering if you could arrange for us all to go to the West Indies, as slaves? I hear the weather is warmer there, they make sure you're fit to work, and you get food and housing free.*

68

The Promised Land

– Morning, Mo.

– *Oh, Hello, Izzy.*

– How're you keeping?

– *I'm making a living.*

– So, what about the news today, then?

– *What news?*

– Haven't you heard?

– *No – I haven't had a chance to look at today's tablets. What's it all about?*

– Only the Promised Land!

– *What do you mean?*

– Well, God's finally announced he's giving us a country of our own.

– *You're joking!*

– Yes – no more wandering!

– *Wow! Really? Frankly, if I have to pull up another tent peg, I'll go meshugana. That's great! So where is it? Italy? I love the food there and it's a beautiful country. Or France? Germany? Did he say?*

– Erm- yes. Apparently, it's somewhere called Israel.

– *Israel – never heard of it. What's it like?*

– Well… I've heard it's quite small.

– *But pretty, eh?*

– Er - kind of – it's mostly desert, they say.

– *So, what about milk and honey?*

– I don't think there's any of them.

– *Hmm – well I suppose we mustn't grumble; so, what are the neighbours like?*

– All Arabs, apparently.

– *Oh well – I'm sure we'll all get on well together.*

– Mmm.

69

Twentieth Century Art

– Hi, Pabs.

– *Oh, buenas dias, Jean-Luc.*

– I see you're still knocking out the old paintings, these days, mate.

– *Yes, sure, why not, as long as they're still selling.*

– Absolutely; why not, eh? And I understand they're fetching even more now than when you and I first met – years ago.

– *It seems so.*

– Hmm... I sometimes wonder about that.

– *Oh, why?*

– Well, come on – you were doing some wonderful stuff back then when we were both youngsters – those nice nudes and wonderful portraits but…

– *I know what you're going to say.*

– Well, the stuff you're doing these days – it's actually crap, isn't it?

– *Yep.*

– So, you agree?

– *Of course, mate.*

– So, what's that all about?

– *OK, I'll tell you, but keep it to yourself.*

– I will.

– *Well, you remember my girlfriend, Jeanne?*

– Give me a break – you've had more girlfriends than I've had hot dinners!

– *Mmm, yes – I admit I do like the ladies.*

– Oh, I know, but what's she got to do with your painting style?

– *Well, you won't remember, but she had a little six-year-old daughter – a lovely little kid, but seriously retarded.*

– Yes?

– *Well, one day I left her in my studio and she started messing about with my paints. When I got back, she'd done a scribble on one of my canvases.*

– So?

– *Long story short, I sold it a week later to an American collector for $50,000, and I've never looked back since.*

70

What's in a Name?

– So, Mr Holmes, first of all, my congratulations on your recent success with the case the press have dubbed 'The Hound of the Baskervilles'.

– *Thank you. I am very grateful for the recognition I have received.*

– Well deserved, I am sure. Moving on, I do appreciate your granting us this very rare personal interview.

– *Well, as you know, I do normally avoid talking to the media.*

– Yes, but, of course, there are many people who follow your cases and are, naturally curious about you as a person.

– *I can understand that.*

– So, may I ask you some more questions beyond the well-publicised details of your cases, documented so well by your associate, Dr Watson?

– *Certainly.*

– Just one question, first of all – how did you come by the name of Sherlock?

– *You told me you wouldn't ask that.*

– Yes, but your fans are, naturally curious.

– *Fuck them!*

– Sorry?

– *It's none of their fucking business!*

– Yes, but...

– *Why does everybody want to take the piss out of my name?*

– I'm sorry, I...

– *The kids at school always called me Shirley or Dreadlock. The little bastards – they had no respect for me as their intellectual superior!*

– I understand that must have been upsetting.

– *And now you're going to take the piss, too!*

– No, no, of course not!

– *You are!*

– No. I assure you, Bollock – oh, sorry.

71

Wise Witnesses

– Well, this was clearly a very nasty crime, and you three seem to be the only ones to have witnessed Mr Gibbon's murder.

– *So it seems.*

– So, let's start from the beginning. Jacko – tell me what you saw.

– *Well, I'd love to be able to help you, but I'd just left the room for a few moments before it happened.*

– I see. So, how about you, Coco?

– *Well, you say someone shouted threats before the shot came, but I didn't hear a thing.*

– I see. So, Peanut?

– *I ain't talking.*

72

Wonderland

– So, what do you think may have triggered these hallucinations in Alice?

– *It's hard to tell.*

– Well, has she been behaving strangely again recently?

– *Not really. I mean she has always seemed a perfectly normal little middle-class girl.*

– Yes, so I understand.

– *She loves her pets – Bunny especially. As an only child, she spends a lot of time with him.*

– Hmm.

– *She loves all kinds of animals, too.*

– Not unlike lots of young children, eh?

– *Yes. I must say – it's a bit more intense, though, with her.*

– How do you mean?

– *Well, she's on her own a lot, and she has a great imagination.*

– How do you mean?

– *Well, she talks to animals as if they are human.*

– Ah, that's sweet – and not unusual.

– *I suppose not.*

– So, what sort of animals does she talk to?

– *Well, apart from Bunny, there's Ches, our cat, and we were at the zoo the other week and she was chatting to hares, flamingos, turtles and dormice.*

– Well, that's what children do.

– *I know, but she seemed to be having actual conversations with them. Afterwards, she seemed almost obsessed.*

– Hmm. I admit, that's a bit worrying.

– *She'll even talk to a caterpillar in the garden.*

– Really! Perhaps you should encourage her to find other interests.

– *We're trying. My husband is teaching her to play chess.*

– That's good.

– *So, we're hoping to prevent her imagination from running wild.*

– Good idea.

– *Yes, she's getting really involved in the chess pieces.*

– Good. So, her behaviour seems pretty normal, these days?

– *Er, yes. I suppose so.*

– But?

– *Well, I'm a bit worried about the small footprints I keep finding on the mantlepiece.*

73

A Stitch in Time

– Well, it's lovely to meet you all, ladies.

– *It's nice to be here on the show.*

– Well, what an achievement, eh?

– *Thank you.*

– So, tell me about it – what gave you the idea?

– *Well, it was Agnes' idea really. She realized that something historic was going to happen, so she got all of us in the embroidery evening class together and off we went down to Hastings – with all our kit, of course.*

– Of course – so you weren't scared?

– *Not really – they were all gentlemen, even knights and, of course, we kept well clear of the heart of the action.*

– It must have been a bit risky, though.

– *Yes – but we felt we had a historic job to do.*

– How right you were – so, how did you go about it?

– *Well, we split up, so that we could cover the whole of the action.*

– I see.

– *And then, as soon as it all went off, we started stitching.*

– It must have been demanding!

– *It certainly was – by the end of the day my sewing finger was red-raw! Pity no-one had invented the fucking camera.*

74

Blessed Cuckoo

– So, how did you get on?

– *No surprise – my camel only had one hoof on the yellow line, so the judge said that the copper was being unreasonable, and he let me off.*

– Great – so are you going back to work straight away?

– *No – I took the morning off.*

– Well, there's another case just starting in Court 2. Fancy going and taking a look?

– *OK.*

– I caught a couple of minutes at the beginning. It's a paternity case.

– *Oh, OK.*

– I'll bring you up to date.

– *OK, but talk quietly.*

– All right.

– *So, who's the angry-looking guy in the overalls, with a pencil and rule in his top pocket, talking to the judge?*

– Oh, he's the husband.

– *Right – and who's the young girl with the baby?*

– Oh, apparently, she's his wife.

– *So, what are the glowing rings she and the baby have got over their heads?*

– Dunno. You know what youngsters are like, these days – fashion fads.

– *Mmm – and that guy in the pinstripe suit, the fedora hat and the pencil-line moustache? The one in the brown and white brogues?*

– Oh, he seems to be the co-respondent. I didn't quite catch his name – J. Hoover or Hover or something.

75

Cold Justice

– All right – put those ski poles down and put your hands behind your back. You're under arrest.

– *Why?*

– You know why, darling.

– *No, I don't!*

– Well, for a start, there's those skis you're wearing – they're obstructing other people.

– *But this is bloody Iceland!*

– Never mind that – and we had to arrest you last week for doing damage with those skates.

– *What damage?*

– It's all on record.

– *This is crazy! All I'm doing is a bit of harmless winter sports!*

– Get in the car.

– *What about my sleigh?*

– The people in the frozen food shop will have it towed.

– *And my horses?*

76

York By-Pass

– Where did you say we're going, Sarge?

– *Dahn the 'ill, son.*

– Bloody 'ell, Sarge – it's taken us over an hour to get up here!

– *So, what else did you 'ave planned for this afternoon, son?*

– I know, but it's bloody tiring, and we're not getting anywhere.

– *So, where else was you thinking of going then? An important social engagement, was it?*

– Well, if you put it that way...

– *I do.*

– Well, at least it's downhill on the way back, but I still don't see the point.

– *You don't 'ave to, son. The Duke knows what he's doing.*

– Well, I'm glad someone does. So, what happens when we get back down there?

– *You'll do as you're told – that's what will 'appen.*

– So what if he tells us to go up again?

– *You'll bloody go, son.*

– I don't get it. Anyway, what are we doing over here in Flanders. Old Boney's done nothing to us.

– *That's none of your business. You just do as you're told, same as me.*

– I hear they say the Duke of York's a coward; is that true?

– *You watch your mouth, son.*

– And I could swear as we got to the top of this hill, I could hear gunfire and see smoke a couple of valleys away, near that little village. What's it called?

– *You mean Waterloo, son?*

– Yes, that's it.

77

A Ripping Yarn

– Hi, Jack.

– *Hi, there.*

– Back in the Big Apple, then?

– *Sure am.*

– So, how was Europe?

– *Not great.*

– Sorry to hear that. You were in London, England, weren't you?

– *That's right. Bit of a dump.*

– So, you didn't enjoy your stay, then?

– *Not really, apart from meeting a few nice young ladies.*

– Oh, that's good. What sort of women? Wealthy?

– *Oh, professional types, all of them.*

– Any long-term relationships?

– *Er, not really. "Ships that pass in the night", but I didn't feel like forming any real relationships. On top of everything else, I was diagnosed as anaemic.*

– Oh, that's rough. What treatment did they suggest?

– *They told me to eat plenty of offal – it's rich in iron, you know.*

– What? Liver and kidneys and stuff?

– *That's it, but you can't get decent fresh meat in the local butchers, where I was, in the East End of London, so I had to make my own arrangements.*

– You had a lot of trouble finding it, then?

– *Yes, it was murder!*

78

A Public Service

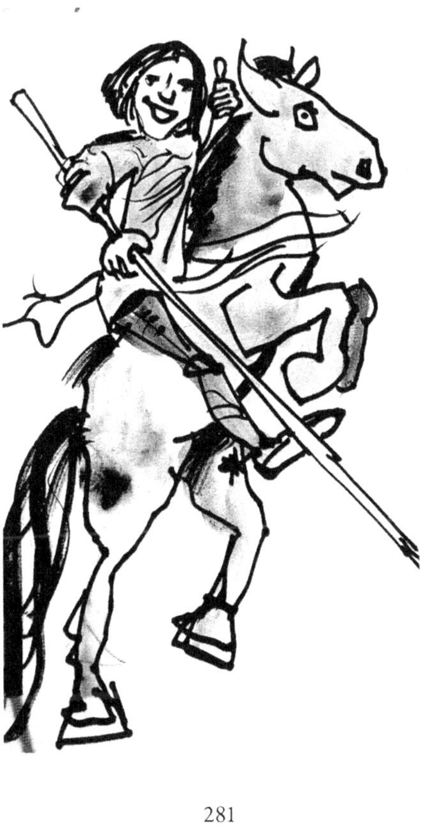

– So, George, you finally killed the dragon – well done!

– *I did.*

– And not a moment too soon, eh? A lot of people's lives will be happier and more relaxed now.

– *I hope so.*

– Oh, they will – we have all been living in fear of the Dragon's wrath for years.

– *I know – me too, to be frank.*

– So, what finally gave you the courage to do it?

– *Oh, I suppose I was desperate. Things kept getting worse and it looked as if nobody else would pluck up the courage.*

– You may be right – but everyone's life will be a lot happier from now on.

– *That's good – it had to be done.*

– You're right. So, now your awful missus is out of the way, what plans have you got?

– *Oh, I suppose I'll carry on doing good works for the Church – if they'll have me.*

– What do you mean?

– *Well, I did murder my wife.*

– What! You're kidding! This is the 4th Century. They'll probably make you a fucking saint, mate – name a day after you!

79

A Pressing Requirement

– So, Mr Caxton, it is rumoured that you have developed a revolutionary press?

– *I certainly have.*

– One which will automate a process which currently involves a high level of laborious activity.

– *Absolutely.*

– particularly, nowadays, the work of monks, like myself.

– *That is so.*

– For which, I must say, we are most grateful.

– *My pleasure.*

– So, I understand that it is not difficult for a new operator to learn to work your new press?

– *I am sure that will be the case.*

– and it will produce perfect results at high speed.

– *That is correct.*

– So, are you able to provide us with a demonstration?

– *With pleasure – follow me,*

– Wow! So, this is it?

– *Yes.*

– Wonderful! So where do you put the grapes in?

80

A Man of Steel

– So, Your Grace, may I first congratulate you on your long and distinguished military and political career.

– *I thank you.*

– Everyone in the land is, of course, in admiration at your historic victory at Waterloo, a turning point in European history.

– *Absolutely, but it was a damn close-run thing.*

– As, I believe, you said at the time, Milord.

– *I believe I did, but I pride myself in dealing with tough challenges.*

– As you say – a triumph of generalship and, if I may say so, of manly determination.

– *And, though I say it myself, of machismo, as they call it these days.*

– Indeed, and, it is clear, you later carried that manly assertiveness into your subsequent political career.

– *I like to think so.*

– Indeed, it is said that you dominated your cabinet and your party with a firm and unrelenting will.

– *Yes – I am, above all, a soldier and a man.*

– Altogether, a record of toughness, dominance and assertion.

– *Indeed.*

– But, may I ask you, as you approach the close of that distinguished career, do you still have any remaining ambitions?

– *Just one.*

– Ah! Can you share it with us?

– *Yes, I'd like to murder that cheeky cunt that first labelled me as an iron!*

Printed in Dunstable, United Kingdom

76045399R00173